BBC

DOCTOR WHO

Big Bang
Generation

BBC
DOCTOR WHO

Big Bang
Generation

Gary Russell

B\D\W\Y
BROADWAY BOOKS
NEW YORK

Copyright © 2015 by Gary Russell

All rights reserved.
Published in the United States by Broadway Books,
an imprint of the Crown Publishing Group,
a division of Penguin Random House LLC, New York.
www.crownpublishing.com

BROADWAY BOOKS and its logo, B\D\W\Y, are trademarks of
Penguin Random House LLC.

This edition published by arrangement with BBC Books, an imprint of
Ebury Publishing, a division of the Random House Group Ltd.

Doctor Who is a BBC Wales production for BBC One. Executive producers:
Steven Moffat and Brian Minchin.

BBC, DOCTOR WHO, AND TARDIS (word marks, logos and devices)
are trademarks of the British Broadcasting Corporation and are used under
license. Bernice Summerfield created by Paul Cornell and used by kind
permission. Peter Guy Summerfield created by Jacqueline Rayner and used
by kind permission. Jack created by Scott Handcock and used by kind
permission. Talpidians created by Simon Barnard and Paul Morris and used
by kind permission.

Library of Congress Cataloging-in-Publication Data is available upon request

ISBN 978-1-101-90581-4
eBook ISBN 978-1-101-90582-1

Printed in the United States of America

Editorial director: Albert DePetrillo
Series consultant: Justin Richards
Project editor: Steve Tribe
Cover design: Lee Binding © Woodlands Books Ltd 2015
Production: Alex Goddard

2 4 6 8 10 9 7 5 3 1

First U.S. Edition

This book is, as promised,
for Dai, Ed, Mike, Andy, James and Richie.
Thanks for a fab Saturday afternoon in Maesteg.

1

Too Much Information

'You sent postcards? To her?'

'I had to get him involved somehow, and you know that just asking him will get you nowhere. And I knew she'd make sure he came. Let's face it, even he never argues with her. Must be the whiskers.'

'That's true, he can be very annoying like that. Won't do the sensible thing, but get a ball of angry fur to yell at him and Bob's yer uncle.'

'Plus, we initially got a bit lost in the time stream, kept popping up for three or four hours in random places. Right basic location and time, but never exactly where we needed to be.'

'And you dragged him to Legion? To home?'

'It seemed a good idea at the time as his being on Earth was clearly interfering with our travelling through time. This seemed neutral. But I think it's gone a bit wrong.'

'You're telling me!' She suddenly reached out for the woman who had surprised her a few moments ago, but instinctively the other woman drew back.

'No touchy-touchy,' she said quickly.

'Sorry. Silly me, I forgot.' She smiled at this. 'It's been a while since I did this voluntarily. And by the way, can I just say, this is convoluted. Even for us, this is convoluted.'

'*I know. I'm sorry. If it helps, let me just tell you that two thousand years from here isn't much fun. It's all a bit boring and the people are snarky – probably because they were expecting a different person altogether. And it's raining. A lot.*'

'And you've got access to time travel.'

'*A time portal; it's not quite the same. Inside a pyramid, which is inside a mountain, on Aztec Moon.*'

'Aztec Moon? You found the Pyramid Eternia? Oh my god, what's it like?'

'*Big. Now far more importantly, I'm here with a number of very dull shouty people from the Church. I'm just hoping that while I'm doing this, talking to you I mean, those same dull people back in the future (ooh, I've always wanted to say that) are still frozen in a handy time eddy or they're going to ask me some very annoying questions when I get back.*'

'I need to get my head around this. You left here and went to the fifty-first century, only to pop back here and ask me to get involved, get him involved, and then go back to the twenty-first century to actually be involved.'

'*Pretty much, yeah.*'

'And you couldn't do it yourself?'

'*Nope.*'

'Why not?'

'*Something happened. The, ummm, rock thing that I dug up on Legion (of all places!) and took to Aztec Moon got a bit damaged and doesn't work that well.*'

'Do you mean the Glamour? You found the Glamour? As well as the Pyramid Eternia? Hell, you found Aztec Moon? That's *amazing!*'

'Can we focus a little bit here, before I cease to exist for all time?'

'Sorry. Yes. That's important too. Absolutely. So, umm, what happened to the Glamour?'

'More a "who" than a "what", I'm afraid.'

She sighed. 'I think I can guess that one.'

'I think you can. So there was just enough power to zap me back from Earth to here, to tell you to go all the way, and then go all the way to Earth and do what I couldn't do because of this time eddy thing.'

'And that's why we need him.'

'He's a Time Lord; he can do whatever it is he does, all Time Lordy, and rescue us. But he needs to go back to where it all went wrong and put it right then. And for that to happen, he sort of needs you.'

'Of course he does.' She sighed. 'What body is he in, by the way? I keep seeing him in the weirdest of orders and it's very confusing.'

'No idea. With any luck, it'll be a new one to me.'

The other woman touched her own hand. It seemed to be fading in and out of existence.

'Hmmm, I think I'm beginning to break up. I really need you to get going or I'm just going to be dispersed into the space-time vortex, and that would be a real shame after everything I've done to avoid that over the years.'

She reached down to the floor and put something down.

It seemed to be a piece of rock, utterly unimpressive, just straightforward rock with maybe a slight white line of crystal threaded through it. She looked up.

'When I'm gone, you're safe to pick it up. Keep it safe and never let it go. It'll take you to me when you are ready.'

'And how will I know when that will be?'

'It reads... signatures, biological signatures. Once everyone that it knows needs to be here, vwoosh, your journey begins.'

'Okaaaay. And again I ask, how will I know when that time comes?'

'You won't. So keep it with you and be prepared. I imagine it will be very soon though. Cos, you know, life's like that. I can't tell you anything more than that.'

'Of course. I know how this works. Sort of. Maybe. Now, look—'

'Listen, if this all goes well, there's something else I need you to do for me. Well, for us I suppose.'

'Which is?'

'Break the First Law of Time. Completely and utterly.'

'Why would I do that?'

'It'll all become clear eventually. I hope. Now then, I think that's everything I needed to say...'

'No, you haven't said anything. Well, nothing that makes sense. You have to tell me about—'

'Sorry, I have to go or I'm going to completely dissipate. And I'd rather try and hold myself together till you get here and put things right.'

She nodded. 'OK, you pop back to the future (I've always wanted to say that, too and I got it right!) and I'll make sure it all goes to plan here.' She peered closer. 'How far from the future are you anyway?'

'*Not much, why?*'

'You look older than I remember.'

'*Cheeky cow!*'

And the other woman vanished.

'You know what? There are days when I just hate my life,' the first woman muttered to no one in particular.

Elsewhere in the universe, things were coming into alignment.

Thousands of years ago, a lump of ordinary-looking rock, threaded through with equally ordinary-looking crystal lattices, fell out of the sky above the planet Earth, hit another piece of rock, did a bit of damage, and got itself buried at the foot of a mountain, observed by a solitary dark-skinned human wearing not very much in the way of clothing bar a small white piece of hide, whose friends hadn't worked out how to invent a calendar yet.

In the early twentieth century, by which time the planet's indigenous population had worked out how to make calendars and used them quite frequently, a German amateur archaeologist and his family were getting off a ship at the Port of Sydney, New South Wales, Australia. They had travelled a long way, for a long time, and were not in the best of moods. The man was nervous, always looking over his shoulder. The woman was just angry at everything. The young son was still amused by something that had happened three days previously. He had started an argument with an English child aboard the ship about some toy soldiers *die Englander* owned and, having lost the argument, proceeded to pick up the victor's toy soldiers and thrown them overboard, where they rapidly sank to the bottom of the South Pacific.

In London, very early in the twenty-first century, an alien from the planet Kadept who really had no right to be on Earth in this time period (he was from six centuries further on and quite a few galaxies across) licked a postage stamp and stuck it on the back of a postcard showing a massive shopping mall on it then popped the postcard into a red pillar box. He stepped back into the road and got clipped by a black cab. He hopped, quite literally, away, clutching his sore bum and yelling some very explicit Kadeptian curse words at anyone who would listen.

In the twenty-seventh century, a ship from the Pakhar BurrowWorld went far beyond the legitimate frontier worlds and arrived on the degenerate backworld of Legion, on the edge of the known galaxies and whatever lay beyond.

In the thirty-sixth century, a group of scholars were arguing about where the ancients of 'the Ancients of the Universe' had been based, what had happened to their technology and whether the legends of the Glamour were true or not. They consulted the writings of Trout the Talpidian; the journals of the Generational Professorial Clone Family of Candy; the mythical Sky Ray Lolly Wrappers of the Miwk Archives; the Holy Dam Scriptures of the Tarka People of Leina VI; the Repository Banks on the Large Moon of Pixlie and even requested access to the Panopticon Records from the Obverse, but got no response.

In the fifty-first century, at Stormcage Confinement Facility Number One, a message was received by a representative of the Church of the Papal Mainframe requesting the loan of a prisoner called Professor River Song. The request was immediately denied.

Also in the fifty-first century, two criminals were sentenced to life without parole at a different Stormcage Confinement Facility, Number Eight. Human con artist Cyrrus Globb had been ensnared by one of his 'conquests', the Spyro weaponista, known to everyone as Kik the Assassin, who had been sent to, well, assassinate him, oddly enough. The Church had managed to arrest both of them on a number of charges and both of them had been imprisoned in adjoining cells to further their humiliation.

And in the TARDIS, as it drifted through the space-time vortex, one of the last survivors of the planet Gallifrey sat reading a dog-eared copy of *The Hungry Tiger of Oz* by candlelight, because he could. It was his TARDIS and if he wanted to have all the lights off and read by candlelight, he would. Could. Should.

Because there was no one else aboard his ship to tell him otherwise.

He was alone.

He was lonely.

He was also, as often happened with him, the reason

all those other things were happening across the past and future, although he hadn't, again as often happened with him, got the slightest clue this was the case.

2

One of Those Days

Sometime in the early part of the twenty-seventh century, after one of a series of galactic wars, a planet on the furthest reaches of, well anywhere really, was colonised, inhabited and civilised.

Frankly, 'civilised' was not a word that was used by those that ended up there – mainly because, after an early attempt to create a city, the rest of the planet went significantly ignored. And partially because the 'dark side' of the planet was dead scary. This was called the 'dark side' because the planet rotated very slowly creating an almost permanent daytime, and thus the 'dark side' only rotated towards the rest of the galaxy once in anyone's lifetime. If they were very old.

And also because no one could be bothered.

Once you had bars, stores and a couple of dodgy establishments that nice people didn't talk about, why bother going beyond Main Street?

So a spaceport, a few bars and stores and an awful lot of criminals were what made the planet well known. That and the fact it was called Legion – not the most hospitable of names for what really was the least hospitable of planets.

Most of the galaxy opted to stay away. Even law-enforcers rarely trekked out there – after all, what was the point. If the people they were pursuing ended up on Legion, they weren't going anywhere else so could be caught on leaving. Or more likely, they'd die in a bar fight, or getting caught in one of the storms that lashed the place ninety per cent of the time.

Now, one of the more popular bars – popular because it had the best beer and the lowest body count – was the White Rabbit. Odd name for a bar but then the owner was pretty odd, so the Doctor had heard.

He was musing on this as he walked up Main Street, dodging an ostrich-sized Land Crow that sped by, its rider clearly drunk and singing loudly. Then the rider fell off, but the Land Crow kept running.

The Doctor was level with the crumpled rider, who was still singing, lying in the mud of the road outside the entrance to the White Rabbit. With a last look at the tuneless wailer, the Doctor pushed the grubby saloon doors apart.

'Well, well, well, look what the cat finally dragged in,' said a high-pitched and rather irritated-sounding voice.

The Doctor looked across the not-terribly-busy bar, and realised the speaker was addressing him.

She was small, about four feet tall, slumped in a stained and cigarette-burned green velvet armchair, a glass of fizzy water in her hand. The Doctor knew that because he knew that these days that was all Ker'a'Nol the Pakhar (Keri to her friends) drank. Ever since… well, that was a whole different lifetime ago. Literally.

To humans, Pakhars tended to resemble giant hamsters – tubby bodies, short arms, slightly longer legs. Their paws were clawed and their noses constantly twitching. Keri's eyes were brown like her fur and she wore a figure-hugging set of combat fatigues (purely casual, she was no warrior – although in a fight, she'd had proven to be quite a good, if noisy, scrapper).

Her left leg was resting on a small occasional table that had been put out especially for her, encased as it was in plaster. A lot of plaster. Clearly Keri had broken her leg.

The Doctor waved an arm around the seriously tacky surroundings they were in. 'Nice place,' he lied.

Keri drained her glass. 'Of all the places to choose, why Legion, yeah?' she asked.

The Doctor sighed. He'd forgotten Keri's little 'yeah?' tick in her speech. It could get very wearing. 'Ummm…' He gave her a quizzical look. 'Ummmm, no, *you* chose it. You wanted to see me.'

Keri Pakhar sank back into her seat with a sigh. 'No Doctor, *you* wanted to see *me*. You sent me a postcard saying you were coming.' Keri reached over to the heavily glass-ringed table and scooped up the card in her paw, waving it at him. 'See? Postcard. Forwarded on from the Mail and Package Archive on somewhere called Ardethe Four – wherever that is. With too little postage on it, by the way, so you owe me money. I had to pay a not-insubstantial fine to collect it. From the Legion Post Office (who knew, they have a Post Office here!). Anyway it wasn't easy. Not with this!' And Keri jabbed the postcard towards her plaster-encased leg..

The Doctor opened his mouth a couple of times, to speak, but then didn't. Instead he knelt down by Keri's leg.

'I wouldn't,' the hamster-like Pakhar hissed. 'You have no idea what's been on that floor. Or indeed what might still be on the floor. The White Rabbit isn't exactly hygienic, yeah?'

The Doctor stared over at the flickering neon sign above the bar – at least two tubes were on the way out. The whole bar was covered with more dust and dirt than the Doctor had seen for a long time. And was that blood on that stool?

In one corner, an old human with no teeth and an old-style prospector's hat was talking to himself and laughing at an imagined joke. The Doctor looked in the other direction. A couple of Killoran mercenaries were getting slowly drunk. Between them, a little scared looking, was a Tahnn rolling an eight-sided die. Platinum-lined credit chips were piled up in front of them. The Tahnn clearly wasn't doing well.

'It hasn't mended?'

'No it hasn't mended.'

The Doctor whipped out his sonic screwdriver.

'Don't you dare,' Keri hissed.

'I just wanted to see if it could help.'

'How is that going to help, yeah?'

The Doctor frowned. 'I don't know. Maybe something has changed the atomic structure of your bones and so the sonic might knit things together faster?'

Keri slumped back in her chair, gripping the big arms in her little paws, trying not to yell at him. After a moment she just smiled. 'You know what you could do for me?'

'What's that?'

'Buy me another glass of water. Dash of lemon.'

The Doctor stood up. 'I'm not here to buy you drinks.'

'Is that because you don't carry money, or because you're just mean?'

He looked shocked. 'Of course I'm not mean. It's just that right now I have better things to do than stand around in bars on Legion, playing servant. To someone who broke their own leg. Being clumsy.'

'I wasn't being clumsy. I was ice skating, yeah.'

'You told me you'd been ice skating before. You said you knew how to ice skate. In fact, you said you were a champion ice skater! So it wasn't my fault you fell over.'

Keri closed her eyes – took a deep breath – then quietly repudiated his facts one by one, counting them off on her claws. 'I told you I went ice skating, yes. I told you I knew enough not to fall over on an ice rink, yes. I actually told you I won a school certificate for ice skating when I was a pup. And yes, it was your fault I fell over because you forgot to tell me that the place we went ice skating wasn't a rink but a living, breathing animal that looked like an ice planet. So when it had a coughing fit I, and everyone else, fell over.'

'I didn't fall over.'

'You were the one making it cough! Of course you didn't fall over.'

The Doctor started walking around the armchair and hen leaned over the top, so Keri had to look straight up, craning her Pakhar neck as best she could. 'Well, that's certainly one way of looking at it and I accept your right to look at it that way, of course.'

'I should have known something was fishy when you told me the planet was called Torvalundeen. How did I not see through that, yeah?'

The Doctor pointed at her. 'Ha! I knew you'd like that. Not many other people there that day got the joke.'

'Not many other people there that day have studied Earth history, so of course they didn't. Who named it Torvalundeen anyway?'

'I did. I mean, you didn't think anyone else out there would make that kind of pun? Its actual name is K-174-B but that's really boring. Well, I think it's boring, so I called it Torvalundeen. It seemed to like the name. And it wasn't coughing, it was laughing.'

'Why was it laughing?'

'Because I told it how I'd given it that name to amuse you.'

'How did it know who Torvill and Dean are? Were? Whatever? It was an alien in another solar system.'

'TV.'

'What?'

'Human TV signals. They go out, into space, for ever. Somewhere in the Kraxis Nebula someone's watching an episode of *Juliet Bravo*. Somewhere a bit closer a couple of Weave are probably watching the first ever *X-Factor* final. And wondering what is going on. So a couple of Olympic ice skaters, well something that clever, that stylish and technically proficient, that gets noticed in the greater universe. Mind you, somewhere out there is a planet that currently thinks The Wurzels on the Christmas Day 1976 *Top of the Pops* is the height of human cultural achievement, so swings and roundabouts.'

Keri looked like she wanted to bang her head on the chair hard, maybe enough to knock herself out. But she didn't, probably because her leg was hurting.

The Doctor reached down and scooped up Keri's tablet that was resting at her hip. He tapped and swiped a few times. 'You have some nice Get Well messages here, very artistic, very… Oh, that one isn't so much artistic as rude. Oh, and I see your Litter Matriarch is still blaming the Pakhar Emperor for everything. Including your leg.'

'She thinks I tripped over a paving slab outside work. That seemed significantly easier than "Yeah, I was on another planet, on an ice rink that was actually a laughing ice monster!" Funny that.'

The Doctor replaced the tablet beside her. 'Never understood Get Well Soon cards. I mean, what are they for? No one's going to send a "Stay unhealthy, please die quickly" card, are they?'

Keri just sighed. She waved the postcard again at him, trying to change the subject. 'So anyway, what did you mean in this card, yeah?'

'What card?'

'This card!' and Keri tossed it at him. Being a postcard, flight was not a skill it possessed naturally, and it merely spun a couple of times and fell limply to the floor in front of him.

'Physical postcards. How quaint.' He picked it up.

> Hope the leg is getting better. On our way soon from the depths of outer space and inner time. Just had tea with Charlie at his investiture.

He looked at the postmark. From 1969. Postage 4d. 'Those were the days.' He sighed. 'So what's with all the space and time stuff?'

Keri bared her teeth. 'Oh, there are times when I could throttle you quite easily. I. Don't. Know. *You* sent it.'

'Did not.'

'It's your handwriting.'

'How do you know that's my handwriting? That looks nothing like my handwriting.'

Keri reactivated her tablet and swiped to a GalWeb mails server page and tapped her account.

The Doctor leaned over again to look, started swiping through, muttering as he did so.

'Gas bill. Electric bill. Credit card bill – what do you spend your money on? Council Tax. Water. Polling Card – don't vote for any of them, least of all her! Would You

Like To Receive Galaxy Five's Reader's Digest For A Year?
The last bastion of print media and no, Keri, you won't
have won ten thousand credits. A private email. Oh, and
another.'

Keri put down the tablet, scrabbled round and produced
two more postcards.

'Two more physical postcards, you are lucky.'

'Read them, yeah.'

The Doctor flipped them over a few times. 'Nice photos,'
he said, but the dark eyes of the Pakhar shrank even more
than normal and, had she had eyebrows, they too would
have narrowed, so the Doctor opted to read, as instructed.
He picked the first:

> Hey you. Coming to visit soon, just as soon as we can get the
> right time stream, don't want to end up in a parallel reality where
> everyone has a horse's head. Mind you, everyone here is wearing
> fluorescent shell suits. 1991 is a bad place to be!

And then:

> Don't worry, not forgotten you (or your poor leg). Picked up
> a nice box of celebratory chocolates from the big new just-
> opened-yesterday Westfield in Shepherds Bush, hope you like
> dark, milk, white and tomato chocolate.
>
> PS: Not sure that *is* tomato chocolate. Not sure tomato
> chocolate is actually a 'thing'. But you never can tell in these
> primitive times and places.

'Do you like tomato chocolate?'

'I don't know what tomato chocolate is and, to be honest, Doctor, I don't think I want to try it very much.'

'Wise move.' He looked back at Keri. 'Why are you showing me these anyway?'

'I want to know why you sent them.'

'And you're wondering where your chocolate is, yes?'

'No, not particularly. It just seems…'

'Yes?'

'Odd. Odd is what it seems. Physical postcards. From. You. When you have the TARDIS. And just where is this Scunthorpe place?'

'I'm really not sure I've ever actually been to Scunthorpe, you know,' he said. 'And whilst that looks a little bit like my handwriting, it isn't. I don't cross my "t"s like that and I can't bear doing little curvy bits under "y"s.'

'So if you didn't send me those postcards, who did?'

'Your Matriarch?'

'If my Matriarch had sent them, they'd be about suing paving stone layers. And they wouldn't have come from Earth.'

'True. How about your lovely old grandad? He's a bit whoop-whoop-whoop…' The Doctor tapped his temple. 'He probably thinks he lives in outer space most days anyway.'

'Oi!'

'Unless…'

'Yes?'

The Doctor stared at Keri for a moment. 'No, no, I'm sure it's nothing.'

'Doctor?'

'Well, I have this friend…'

Keri sighed. 'I can see the quote marks around "friend" from here.'

'No, no, she really is a friend. An old friend. Well, not old like your grandad – no one's that old – but a friend from a long time ago. And that might be her handwriting. I actually think you've met once or twice. I don't recall how well you got on.'

'I rarely get on with your friends Doctor. More often than not they try to kill me. Or, in the case of your old tin dog, shoot me.'

'Well, to be fair to K-9, you were possessed by the ancient spirit of the Kortha Gestalt. Sarah Jane and Luke did explain to me that you weren't best pleased, though…'

'Anyway, moving to the here and now, just how did this particular "old friend" know I'd broken my leg, yeah?'

'Ah yes, that might have something to do with Gal-Tube.'

'And my leg-breaking incident was on that, I'm guessing. Humiliation on a universal scale.' Keri paused. 'Who uploaded it, Doctor?'

'Anyway, so it's possible that she saw it and decided to make her way here, to see you. And maybe me. It's been a lot of years and faces since we last met up. Well, I'd better head off.'

'Oh no you don't. If someone I don't know from your past is coming here, you're sticking around too.'

'I am?'

'You are. But before she gets here, you're also going to explain why you uploaded footage of me falling on my bum to the entire universe, yeah?'

The Doctor smiled. 'Fizzy water, yeah?'

3
Be My Icon

The human colony of El Diablo was established in the late forty-ninth century, on the outskirts of the Vadim solar system, right at the heart of the human empire's trade routes. El Diablo was named because of its dichotomous sulphurous atmosphere and volcanic polar regions, which put a lot of settlers off – its distance from its sun didn't help.

But enterprise can be found everywhere and one of the fledgling power companies, a small mom-and-pop family operation, decided to invest in the dwarf planet, seeing if it could contain the unpleasant lava seas and turn that into self-perpetuating power to keep a colony going, rather like being a planet and sun all in one.

After many years of planning and experimenting and some very hard-sought patents, the company succeeded and began selling plots of terraformed land on this exciting, potentially prosperous new world.

And that's when the big corporations moved in – not worried about the dwarf planet itself, but terribly interested in the technology and patents owned by the family business. Without too much concern for the people involved, one of the bigger companies, Bolen, simply absorbed the company in a hostile takeover, sacked the family, and owned El Diablo outright.

Within a hundred years, with the technology having proved functional and successful, Bolen began populating El Diablo with businesses – mainly banking, securities, and a few satellite offices of the bigger cosmo-nationals. And a lot of coffee shops.

But as always when you mix big business with financial institutions (and a ready supply of coffee) the less-than-honest types move in. Not exactly crime lords and gangsters, but a significant number of small time grifters and con artists who saw an opportunity to make a quick buck out of shady transactions, then move on, perhaps to the gallery world of Rembrandt or the jewellery world of Sappho – lots of easy pickings from the celebs, aristocracy or other delusional inbreds with a shared IQ of six that populated such places.

Bolen, however, wanted to stop these stings occurring, so they went to the Church of the Papal Mainframe and signed up for their security and other services.

Thus it came to pass in the early summer of 5064 that a man as wide as he was tall (and he was quite tall) called Cyrrus Globb arrived on El Diablo. Globb probably wasn't his real name – rather as Al Capone had been called Scarface or George Nelson was called Babyface because of physical characteristics, so Globb had become known as exactly that thanks to his impressive bulk. He also, it had to be noted, moved very fast and quietly for a man of said shape and size.

So Globb became a grifter, a conman and a rogue. There's often a charm, a slight admiration of someone who can steal millions of currency by swindling someone more stupid and gullible and rich and (usually) unpleasant. They become sort of modern Robin Hoods (although not so much redistributing the wealth to the poor as redistributing it more through their own tax havens).

The drawback for someone like Globb was that people often don't like being swindled, especially if, along with the money or the goods (or both), they also lose face with their peers and family.

The result of a successful criminal career is often an equally impressive bounty placed upon them, and in Cyrrus Globb's case, the emphasis was on the DEAD part of WANTED DEAD OR ALIVE.

Enter a slim, muscular lady from the planet Spyro, famed for her ability to always get whatever she was paid to get, and also for having hollow telescopic bones, which meant she could usually get in and out of places few others could. She was known universally as Kik the Assassin – if that was her name, no one knew. She was a weaponista, meaning that there were no weapons in the known universe, past and present, that she didn't have an instinctive ability to use to absolute perfection. As a result, she was very highly regarded and very highly paid. Most people were also utterly terrified of her – it was said that if a lean, powerful reptile lady with turquoise skin, a short silver Mohawk and pupil-less yellow eyes was standing before you, you were probably already dead and your brain hadn't registered yet.

And that falling sensation, that sound in your ears of a roar like the sea, and that blur of movement as the ground seemed to be reticulating was your brain finally going, 'Oh, damn, I've just been killed by this corner of the universe's foremost weaponista, Kik the Assassin.' Although to be honest, the brain only got as far as 'Oh damn, I've—' before shutting down.

Therefore when one of the small but respected-in-dodgy-circles cartels on El Diablo took umbrage at Cyrrus Globb casually relieving them of two years' profits in exchange for a suitcase not of neutron plasma tubes but of common-or-garden bricks, they paid Kik the Assassin handsomely to rid the universe of Globb.

Globb, perhaps sensibly, rarely stayed put for long and it was actually 5066 before Kik the Assassin (now quite rich because her monthly retainer was nothing to be sniffed at) tracked Globb down.

He was on Mason's World, a popular casino and leisure planet and he foolishly stopped for one last whisky one night, offered to buy one for 'the pretty blue-ish lady beside me' and found himself facing the wrong end of a number of weapons.

Ironically for Globb, rescue arrived in the form of the Church – a Verger-led troop took out the door, the windows and a significant number of tables and chairs while entering the bar to arrest him. And Kik the Assassin, not possessing a death wish, surrendered immediately.

Six weeks later, the swiftest judgment ever came back from the courts of El Diablo: Globb was sentenced to life and Kik the Assassin, who was a bit cleverer at covering her tracks that night, got a three-month sentence for carrying an unlicensed firearm – the rest were all licenced, because she was too good at her job for them not to be. Almost. She was pretty sure this was a frame-up, but what's three months when the average Spyro lifetime is 450 years?

Thus it came to pass that the Church of the Papal Mainframe saw fit (or maybe some governor with a delicious sense of humour and irony) that Cyrrus Globb and Kik the Assassin were placed in adjoining cells. And, like all the cells on this Stormcage facility, the walls were merely force fields and the two could sit and glower at one another all day long.

One day, salvation presented itself in the form of a Headless Monk who came bearing a letter – a real, honest to goodness paper, handwritten and sealed with candle wax letter – for each of them.

Kik the Assassin read hers, written in the finest Spyro fractal fonts, with a huge grin on her face.

Globb read his, written in block capitals in green ink, with a scowl.

When they looked up, the Headless Monk was gone, his task done.

A moment later, their cell doors deactivated and they both walked out. Two guards were in the corridor, chatting about wives, dinners, cricket – who knew or cared? The important thing was that although they saw their two prisoners escaping, they did nothing about it. This was probably because of the wad of cash the Headless Monk had given each of them a few moments earlier.

Outside the Stormcage was a small two-person shuttle. Wordlessly, they got into it, Kik the Assassin expertly gunning the propulsion unit, and off they soared into space.

Only then did Globb speak. 'It says you aren't allowed to kill me, and this contract negates and invalidates all and any others you have regarding me.'

Kik the Assassin smiled and nodded. 'I understand that too. It also stated that when this is over, I am to return you here, alive and unharmed and if I do, I get a pardon. If I don't, they'll kill me.'

'I thought no one could kill you,' Globb said.

She smiled again. 'If a Headless Monk tells you he'll kill you, I have little doubt that his order are the only people in this galaxy that can do exactly that. I have no desire to die or remain in captivity, so we're doing this job, getting back here with you safely in tow, and then I go home.'

'And what if I don't want to come back with you? What if I decide that a life on the run is better than a life back there?' He thumbed in the general direction of the Stormcage.

Kik the Assassin passed over her letter. 'Paragraph three.'

Globb looked at it. 'I can't read this gibberish.'

Kik the Assassin sighed, snatching the letter back and

pushing it against a small screen on the systems console of the ship. Immediately a hologram of the letter appeared in the air. 'Earth English. For beginners,' she snapped.

Immediately Globb could read it. Paragraph three made it quite clear what would happen to Globb, courtesy of the Headless Monks (something about his joining their order permanently), and Globb nodded. 'Stormcage it will be.'

'Don't you get a reduced sentence, though?'

Globb shrugged. 'A decade suspended. Time to try and get away, I suppose.'

'From them? Good luck trying.'

They remained sat in silence for the rest of the journey as they plotted and schemed about how to do exactly what was required of them according to their letters.

Which was to go to a planet neither of them had heard of called Aztec Moon and steal an ancient artefact from under the noses of another part of the Church of the Papal Mainframe. Weird, but neither of them felt like arguing with the Vatican.

'A door! We have found a door!'

It was a massive door – that was a fact no one could argue with. Not the military specialists, the learned explorers or even the shuttle crew could find any reason to argue with Professor Horace Jaanson's proclamation.

'You're quite right,' muttered Colonel Sadkin. 'That is, indeed, a door.'

'What's really fascinating is that it's a door created by a civilisation vastly different to ours. A whole species created that door leading to heaven knows where and we are here. Now. Today. Ready to open it and explore the unknown.' Professor Jaanson smiled at Sadkin, as if that made everything all right with the world.

He was an annoying little man, Sadkin had decided about a week ago. When he had arrived at the Mainframe, along with his weird little alien helper, Jaanson had looked like he'd stepped out of a historical movie – he wore a tweed jacket, tweed plus fours, massive boots and a ridiculous tweed deerstalker that made his whole ensemble look as if he were going for a grouse-shoot on one of the Aristocracy Planets rather than exploring a damp, icy, muddy barren place like this. It appeared he had a wardrobe of identical clothes as that was all he'd been seen wearing ever since.

Colonel Sadkin sighed and looked behind him. His Clerics, the Vergers and, standing right back by their shuttle, the two pilots – although they were already bored by the door and had started tapping away on their tablets, no doubt on some social networking site, trying to find company for the night.

Not that anyone was likely to make a trip to Aztec Moon, even for the dubious delights of the two pilots. It was, frankly, a dull planet with large mountains of russet-coloured rock and a couple of local stars that lit the place up moodily. At one point, as the shuttle had buzzed through the atmosphere, they'd spotted a silvery lake lined with more rocks. The colour of the stone had earned the place its name: Aztec Moon.

At least that was what people knew it as. Its true name was Bates's World, named after some explorer who had discovered it years back. But Sadkin had always heard that – as no one liked the mysterious Bates that much – when humanity came to map it out and discovered that the reddish rock made it look like seas of blood from the upper atmosphere, tales of the violent South American ancient society had been cited and Aztec Moon had stuck as its name.

Right now, the Colonel decided, no matter how exotic or poetic Aztec Moon sounded, it couldn't disguise the fact it was raining. Hard.

The Colonel adjusted his iVisor and scanned the doorway. It was cut into the side of a large obsidian pyramid, carved from some rock that evidently wasn't part of the natural landscape of the planet. It was decorative but that gave no suggestion as to why it was there. But it was the only sign so far that Aztec Moon had ever had visitors before, or indigenous people – perhaps they had built it. 'Indigenous.' Colonel Sadkin hoped he'd used the right phrase – he had overheard Jaanson and his Talpidian digger say it earlier. The image in his iVisor ran through the spectrum waveforms, searching for evidence of recent activity, dangerous substances or just anything other than dark rock.

What he suddenly saw, making the doorway flash in his iVisor with a purple glow, made him physically step back.

He swung his blaster up, cocking it. Without waiting to be told, his six men did the same.

The sound of this drew Jaanson and his Talpidian assistant's attention to them. Even the shuttle pilots looked up, albeit only briefly, at this.

'Colonel?' the Talpidian nervously stammered, blinking its pink eyes and rubbing its whiskers, as it always did whenever something alarmed it. 'What is the problem?'

Sadkin pointed at the door. 'That is. It's not a door.'

'It most certainly is a door,' whined Jaanson. 'You can plainly see it's a door. A door for a giant, yes – you would need to be over thirty feet tall just to reach the handle, but it is still a door.'

'A door,' confirmed the Talpidian.

Sadkin waved his Clerics and Vergers backwards, then reached forward and rudely yanked Jaanson towards him. Jaanson opened his mouth to complain, but Sadkin told him to shut up.

The Talpidian scurried over, its mole-like nose scrunching up, smelling. 'I smell danger,' it finally said.

For the first time Jaanson took things seriously. 'OK, Colonel, tell me what the problem is.'

'How long have you been searching for this place?'

Jaanson took a deep breath, like he was delivering a lecture. 'The Ancients of the Universe, it is believed, once seeded the universe, bringing life. Akin to the Prometheans. The Kokopellian Republic. The Corcini. The—'

The Talpidian nudged Jaanson. 'Professor, I think the representative of the Papal Mainframe requires the... the edited version.'

Jaanson harrumphed, annoyed at not being able to deliver his full thesis. 'Basically, Colonel Sadkin, it is considered by many esteemed academics and indeed your own theo-logicians of the Vatican, that life in this quadrant of space, possibly the entire known universe, may have started here. The Ancients of the Universe have been an obsession of mine all my life. Many expeditions have been here; none has even found this door before, let alone come up with answers.'

The Colonel waved towards the pyramid's door with his blaster. 'And you're the lucky one who finally did so, yeah?'

The Professor nodded eagerly. 'That's why I contacted the Papal Mainframe. I had worked out that everyone has always been on the dry side of Aztec Moon. But by coming here, to the damp side, I knew my calculations were more accurate than theirs. Generations of explorers wasted their lives – Kos Elwyn, the Brotherhood of Logicians, Holoon-Igma, Bates himself – and even that ridiculous fool Melville Trout – none of them realised it was here, exactly opposite to where they were looking!'

'Where's your expert?'

Jaanson looked affronted. 'Expert? I am the expert!'

The Talpidian nudged Jaanson. 'He means the archaeologist.'

'Yeah, where is she?'

Jaanson shrugged. 'She was supposed to be here hours ago. Ridiculous, you ask for an archaeologist with a penchant for not observing the rules, and they're late!'

Colonel Sadkin ignored this – deliberately. The less he

knew about this Professor Song (and the dubious things she was reported to have done) the better – leave that to Colonel Octavian, the Father of the Chapel charged with looking after her. Instead he yelled out to one of his men. 'Verger Brown, get the shuttle pilots ready to leave. We're going.'

Brown dutifully dashed off.

Horace Jaanson was having none of it. 'Colonel, your orders—'

'My orders were to bring you here and look after you, providing there was no danger.' He again jabbed his blaster at the door. 'That says "danger" to me.'

'Why?'

Sadkin passed his iVisor, and Jaanson swiped it, placing it over his angry eyes. His head went up and down a couple of times, tracing the height of the door in a series of nods. He adjusted the iVisor a couple of times.

Sadkin just smiled at him. 'See what I mean?'

Jaanson slowly shook his head. 'But that's why I needed my expert archaeologist. This confirms what I knew!'

Sadkin finally lost his temper. '*You knew?*' A couple of his men took a step back in shock. 'You knew this wasn't a door but the entrance to a time portal?'

'I assumed so, yes. It would explain so much about the mystery. I theorised that the Ancients didn't just die out – they deliberately vanished, went into a time portal. Hopefully this will tell us where or when. And where they took the Glamour.'

'The what now?'

Jaanson looked at the Colonel in anger, passing – well throwing, really – back the iVisor. 'Didn't you read my books, my papers? Why did you come if you are so ignorant of what we will discover here?'

'I was assigned. Period. End of. I certainly didn't choose to come to a blood-coloured, wet, cold, windy and smelly rock with you and your oversized mole.'

'Talpidian,' corrected the Talpidian. 'Although I know a lot of humans who make that assumption…'

Jaanson waved him quiet. 'Yes, Colonel, I believe this is the access to the Pyramid Eternia – the housing to a time portal. That's why I wanted Professor Song sent here. They say she has experience with time travel.'

'It's also probably why she's always locked in a Stormcage,' Sadkin countered. 'Knowing her reputation, she's probably already escaped en route.'

'That would be most irritating,' Jaanson muttered. 'I need an experienced archaeologist used to dealing with the unusual and unexplained.'

'Hullo there,' yelled a new voice.

Jaanson, Sadkin and the Clerics all turned to look at where the voice came from. Even the pilots stopped swiping their tablets again.

Sadkin frowned. On a rocky outcrop about forty feet away were four… people.

The person who had yelled, a human dark-haired woman, dressed in fatigues (but not Cleric ochre, more two-tone black and grey) was waving. Next to her, was a smaller creature in a hooded sweatshirt. Next to that was a young dark-skinned human in similar clothes to the older woman, and finally a weird alien with a pointed chin, red eyes and legs like a grasshopper (otherwise, basically humanoid). He raised his hand and feebly waved too.

'Hi,' he added. 'Sorry to butt in and all that.'

'Who the hell are you?' Jaanson yelled.

The woman jumped down and started walking towards the group. Her friends remained where they were, although Sadkin could see the young, hooded one tense slightly, as if anticipating trouble. Fast and sharp, that one, the Colonel thought. He also noted that they all wore backpacks that seemed a tad heavier than normal archaeological equipment would require. He flicked his eyes to Cleric Elias and back at the hooded thing. With a nod only Sadkin could see, Elias made his focus the hooded creature.

'I must repeat the Professor's question,' Sadkin said. 'This is an official Papal Mainframe excursion. I am Colonel Sadkin, Father of this Chapel.' He indicated his Clerics and Vergers. 'Why are you here?'

The woman didn't speak again until she was right up close to the Colonel, all smiles. She held out a hand, and Sadkin rather surprised himself by shaking it.

'Professor Bernice Summerfield,' she said. 'How do you do.' She looked over to Jaanson and the Talpidian.

'And?' Jaanson demanded.

'I'm an archaeologist, but probably not the one you were expecting.'

4

Of Crime and Passion

The planet Legion, and its capital, curiously called Legion City, was, the Doctor decided, a strange place. He was quite familiar with edge-of-the-known-galaxy planets; places where only the very brave, the very foolhardy, the very criminal or (more often than not) the very drunk found themselves.

He was also very familiar with planets that were, frankly, made up of a few stores and bars and places of less salubrious occupancy that seemed to thrive on the outskirts of civilisation. Its nearest synonym in human culture would be the American 'Wild' West of the mid-nineteenth century. Legion City could just as easily be Tombstone or Dodge City if it weren't for the spaceport, the flashing neon signs, the constant drizzle and the variety of alien species carrying ever more outrageous weaponry to 'protect' themselves.

Apparently there was even a Chief of Security here, like an old Wild West Marshal, but the Doctor hadn't seen any sign of that. Despite, he noted, having witnessed three bar brawls in the White Rabbit alone – and the Rabbit wasn't the only bar here by any means.

He was using his smartphone to access information about the place. It was, frankly, sketchy. Keri had told him that one of the reasons Legion was a popular destination for the disenfranchised was its anonymity. What happens on Legion stays on Legion. Often in a shallow, unmarked grave.

Legion City was certainly its only city, but there were other smaller villages and shanty towns on the 'light' side of the world. Legion wasn't a huge planet (more a planetoid really, maybe even a moon) except that it didn't revolve around a sun – it was simply too far away. It was one of those rare places that actually stood still. Well, it probably didn't, but its orbit took nearly a lifetime for the average being just to shift from summer to autumn so to all intents and purposes, it never moved.

It was cold and perpetually dusk – again, because the sun was a loooong way away.

It also meant that it had a dark side, literally, the side that faced 'the unexplored universe'. Over the decades since the planet was 'civilised', stories had grown up about the dark side, rumours that it was populated by demonic evil beings who would eat the soul of anyone going there.

The Doctor was quite intrigued by this. As he'd got older, he'd got more daring. Three or four regenerations ago, visiting somewhere like Legion would have been nowhere on his agenda. These days, he quite liked living dangerously. After all, if you're going to be over two thousand years old, you need a bit of excitement, a bit of a thrill to keep you feeling alive, avoid retreading the same old adventures and holidays that he'd had around his fourth or fifth regenerations.

Of course, right now he had no idea how long he was going to be on Legion at all. Keri was unclear as to whether the postcard-sender that had brought them together here wanted them to wait or what they intended.

And the Doctor had itchy feet – he needed to get moving.

So he made a decision. He'd given Keri one of his seemingly innumerable cell phones. He'd picked up a job lot in Houston recently in exchange for helping a man solve a problem with a rather large mouse that may or may not have come from the planet Vermia a hundred years earlier and been asleep.

So, while he stood on the street outside the White Rabbit, marvelling at the domestication of the Land Crows, he had his sonic screwdriver in his hand, zapping one of these cell phones, giving it universal roaming and linking it automatically to the TARDIS and a phone he himself had started carrying a few months ago when he and his friend Clara had got separated at a Sam Smith concert. Having sorted the phone, he slipped it into a pocket and flipped his sonic screwdriver in his hand, like a gunslinger, ending in a pose like said gunslinger.

At which point a very tall, very muscular bright pink reptile tapped his shoulder. It looked rather like an upright crocodile, from a Disney cartoon.

'Mine,' it said.

The Doctor shook his head. 'I don't think so, friend. Mine.'

The pink reptile held out its hand. 'Mine. Pretty green stick. Mine.'

The Doctor just smiled. 'I think if it was yours, it'd would have already been in your hand. The fact that it's in my hand would suggest that it is, absolutely and irrefutably, mine. Goodbye.'

Turning his back, he would later be told by Keri the Pakhar, was not considered good form by the Kenistrii. He would also be told that the Kenistrii were pretty famous for disembowelling their victims and eating them raw.

Therefore as he turned away from this big pink crocodile, its mighty paw slammed into his back, sending him crashing into the muddy roadway.

'Mine,' it said with such a significant amount of menace and teeth-baring that the Doctor had to wonder if it might be a good idea just to give over the sonic and get the TARDIS to create a new one.

A crowd gathered around the two of them, obviously expecting a fight. Indeed the Doctor could clearly see a number of bewhiskered and toothless old prospector-types taking bets from one another.

Nice. Clearly the pink crocodile was odds-on to win.

'Why do you want it?' he gasped at the alien.

'Mine.'

'I think we've established that isn't really true. But I do acknowledge you'd like it to become yours. Tell me why.'

'Mine.'

The Doctor blew air out of his cheeks as he got up. This really wasn't going to be easy. He flipped the sonic once again, and then tossed it over to the alien. 'Yours,' he agreed with a tight smile.

The Kenistrii clearly couldn't believe his luck, then grabbed the Doctor in a big hug, nuzzled him and walked away with his prize.

As the disgruntled grumbling crowd separated, arguing about their betting not resulting in an eating, the Doctor could see Keri, on a crutch, standing in the doorway of the White Rabbit.

As much as it was possible for a four-foot-nothing giant hamster to register a mixture of weary annoyance and resigned pity, Keri shook her head. 'Seriously, you've nothing better to do than challenge a Kenistrii hatchling, yeah?'

'I didn't challenge him...' the Doctor protested. 'He started it!'

'Whatever.' Keri hobbled back inside and the Doctor followed, fetching the phone for her.

She took it, sniffed it and tapped the screen, staring at the apps that flashed up. 'And I have this because?'

'Because we can stay in touch, no matter how far apart we are. Which, if I'm honest, I'm rather hoping will be quite far. Not that I don't like you...'

'You don't, much.'

'But mainly because I'm not keen on staying on Legion.'

Keri nodded. 'I get that. By the way, have you really just

put something as dangerous as a sonic screwdriver in the hands of a child, yeah?'

The Doctor brought his own smartphone out of his pocket and showed Keri his apps. He tapped one called FIND YOUR SONIC.

'Seriously?' asked Keri. 'Who creates an app that only you can use?'

He smiled. 'My friend Clara got her friend Shona to make it.'

Keri looked at the little logo. 'Shona is a 12-year-old human girl, yeah?'

'What makes you say that?'

'The logo has Poyo Satou on it.'

'Maybe I like cats.'

Keri looked at him. 'You don't even know who Poyo is, do you?'

'She's a cat.'

'No, he is a cat.' Keri shivered. 'Cats. Horrible things.' Keri activated the app and sure enough, less than half a mile away, a little blip told them both where the Doctor's sonic was. The Doctor tapped on the app, opened another menu and selected 'Deactivate Battery'. After a few seconds, the sonic stopped bleeping. Another menu: 'Deactivate sonic'. He tapped that. 'Your Kenistrii is now the proud owner of a useless metal stick,' he said. 'This app is very handy when I lose sonic screwdrivers. Or have them stolen.'

'Happens a lot, doesn't it?'

'More than you'd expect,' the Doctor conceded.

'At which point both their phones bleeped with an INCOMING TEXT envelope emblem.

'That was fast,' Keri said, tapping her phone. 'Who did you give these numbers to, yeah?'

The Doctor read the message aloud. 'Run out of postcards and stamps. Meet me in Sydney, New South Wales, 2015. Bring the TARDIS, we may need the old girl. Happy Christmas xx.' He frowned. 'Meet who?'

'No number recognised,' Keri said. 'You'd better go.'

'Why? I'm not just running off at the first mysterious message I get.'

'Two reasons,' Keri smiled. 'One, it's a mystery – we both love a mystery – and now I have a phone, you can keep me abreast of things. Maybe I can help – if that has 8G activated, I could do what I do best and research things for you.'

'And the other reason?'

'In about four minutes a pretty angry pink Kenistrii is going to come looking for you to turn his sonic screwdriver batteries back on. If you say no, he may well try and take *your* batteries out, yeah?'

The Doctor thought about this. 'I like your reasoning,' he said. He waved his smartphone. 'Speak later.'

'Bye Doctor,' Keri said, shooing him away.

Before the Doctor was out of the door, Keri was on GalFaceTweet, letting all her friends know she'd scored a new phone with universal roaming, with data charges that the Doctor was going to be responsible for.

As the Doctor crossed the street, he re-read the message.

There was something familiar in the tone of the postcards, of this text, a familiarity with him that he couldn't place.

Before he could think too much more about it, he saw an angry pink crocodile stomping towards him. Worse, it had brought mom and pop crocodile, twice the height, twice as angry.

'I really don't like this place,' he muttered as he got into the TARDIS and headed for Earth in the twenty-first century.

5

Read My Lips

Professor Bernice Summerfield, adventurer, archaeologist, lecturer, occasional time traveller (but not so much these days) and most importantly, mother to:

Peter Guy Summerfield. Half-human, half-Killoran (big tall aliens that look like anthropomorphised Rottweilers; smarter than they look and quite charming). Typical teenager, moody, often hates his mum, wants his dad around, gay, looking for a boyfriend, really good with guns. Starting to become really friendly with:

Ruth (not her real name). Early twenties, a bit naive at times, comes from a far-off planet where her parents were super-rich royalty and really not terribly nice. Nor was Ruth who, when with them, was your archetypical spoilt-princess type. Her mind was wiped during an attempt to flee from an uprising and she has absolutely no memory, or traits, of her previous life before she met Bernice, who introduced her to:

Jack (absolutely his real name, he has no surname). Kadeptian ambulance-chaser-type lawyer, not his family's most favourite son (there were a lot of sons, to be the least favourite was a big, if not good, achievement), who met Bernice on a weirdly distorted future Earth that was actually like Victorian London, where he got known as Spring-Heeled Jack. Has long, grasshopper-like legs, red eyes, pointed chin and ears and is quite foppish and urbane. He's also engaged to Ruth. Awwww.

That was not quite how Bernice introduced her team to Professor Horace Jaanson, Colonel Sadkin and everyone else. It was along those lines but a bit punchier, and she didn't mention the Peter being gay and looking for love bit because it wasn't hugely relevant and the last time she had described him as such – to a rather elegant young Halantii in the bar of the White Rabbit on Legion, Peter had got moodier and grumpier and didn't speak to her for a week. Bernice was indeed a typical mother, just a bit out of practice.

'How did you get here?' was Colonel Sadkin's not entirely unjustified question.

'Would you believe, this bit of rock –' she held up the rock given to her some days earlier – 'sort of homed in on this place once my guys were all together in the bar one night. We didn't get a lot of choice, or time to pack a toothbrush, so excuse us for not being prepared. One minute we're chatting to one another; the next – whoosh, here we are twenty-something centuries into our own future.'

'No,' said Colonel Sadkin. 'I wouldn't believe that one bit.'

'For one thing,' Professor Jaanson piped up, 'time travel is impossible.'

Bernice looked at the group around and settled on Colonel Sadkin. There was something in his eyes…

'Oh that's not true at all,' Bernice countered. 'As the Colonel here knows full well.'

The Professor turned to the Father of the Chapel. 'Colonel?'

'Time travel is known to exist, in a limited form, to very special individuals.'

'Consider me, us, special individuals then,' Bernice said, adding before anyone else could speak: 'Now, I think we need to get inside that big polyhedron thing and see what's inside, don't you?'

'What polyhedron?'

'The Pyramid Eternia, which contains what you are searching for. The time portal. Belongs to the Ancients of the Universe.' She smiled sweetly at Jaanson. 'Do keep up, Professor. I thought this was your speciality?'

'How do you know who I am?'

'She reads a lot. And listens rather than talks,' Peter said, pulling his hoodie back, revealing his human/canine face. A couple of the Church took an involuntary step back, although Brother Elias remained focused on him, as per his orders.

'This is all getting a little tense,' Jack said. 'Why don't we all just calm down and get along, yes? We all want the same thing.'

'Which is?'

'To get in there, I'm guessing?' Jack threw a quick look to Bernice, making sure that was indeed what she wanted.

She smiled back. 'Jack's right, we're not in competition. I think we can help you get inside, Professor. That's what you wanted an archaeologist for, wasn't it?'

'I didn't want or need anyone,' Jaanson said petulantly. 'The Church insisted on it.'

'Well, now you have me,' Bernice said agreeably. 'Oh, hullo,' she added, waving at the Talpidian digger who was trying to look insignificant behind the Professor. 'Smelled anything dangerous yet?'

The Talpidian nodded.

'Of course he has,' the Professor said unkindly. 'That's all he ever does. Smell danger and make everyone nervous.'

'Then why's he here?' Bernice asked.

'I need a good digger,' the Professor replied. 'Not that it's any of your business.'

Ruth offered her hand to the Talpidian, deliberately knocking the Professor out of the way. 'It's an honour to meet such a loyal and smart person,' she said. 'Talpidians are my favourite people in the galaxy.'

The Talpidian immediately went bright pink and looked away nervously. 'Thank you,' he said finally.

'Tell me what you've discovered here so far,' Ruth said, easing him further away from the group.

Colonel Sadkin sidled closer to Bernice. 'Clever move,' he muttered.

Jack and Peter were now following Ruth's lead and

personally introducing themselves to the Clerics, shaking hands, patting shoulders, that sort of thing.

'My team are experts,' she replied. 'And not the enemy.' She nodded towards Jaanson who was switching his point of view between the retreating digger and the Church soldiers, who were doing nothing.

'Why are you letting us be split up?' Jaanson exploded.

'He's a liability,' Bernice muttered to Sadkin.

'He's also paying good money. Well, his Academy is.'

'The people who need to pay good money for something like this are usually the least qualified to actually do it. He probably got where he is today by shouting a lot.'

'He is an expert on the Ancients.'

'Where I come from, anyone who knows *anything* about history can be an expert on the Ancients. There's not much to learn. There is, however, a lot you can *pretend* you have discovered, to make yourself sound important.'

Sadkin smiled at her finally. 'And you, Professor Summerfield? Do you do much to make yourself sound important?'

'All the time, Colonel. It creates an air of mystery. I learned that one from the best.'

'I should probably just arrest the lot of you.'

'Probably. But I think you want to find out why you've been dragged here as much as I do. And I am actually capable of opening that door. Unlike Professor Jaanson.'

'Two Professors. That's two too many for me at the best of times. This isn't the best of times.'

'Call me Benny, then. It's a lot easier. When people call

me "Professor", I spend a few seconds looking around me expecting someone like Jaanson to be who they actually want.' She held out her hand.

Sadkin weighed this up and then shook it for a second time. 'OK, Benny it is. Just be aware. I don't trust you. I may quite like you, but I don't trust you.'

'That's cool I'm used to that. The no-trust bit, I mean.'

The Colonel was looking over Bernice's shoulder. 'What about her? Do we trust her too?'

'What "her"?' Bernice turned to look behind her, where Sadkin was pointing. There was a lithe blueish woman with a silver mane of hair, seemingly trying to get her bearings. Bernice couldn't tell if she'd yet spotted her and the Colonel.

'Oh, her? Her, I don't know. But if she's not with me and not with you, maybe she's with him.'

It was Colonel Sadkin's turn to look elsewhere. 'No, he's not with the Church.'

'He doesn't look it, to be frank,' Bernice said.

They were watching a large human striding towards the pyramid, oblivious to the Church-with-added-Summerfield group.

The blueish woman skittered across the russet terrain after him, and it seemed certain she hadn't seen them either.

Bernice waved Peter over and he came. He too had spotted the newcomers.

'Not sure I like this, Mum,' he said. 'Too many variables.'

'"Variables"?' asked Sadkin.

Bernice nodded. 'Yeah, we were expecting Professor Jaanson and probably a small party of religious students, like a Sunday School outing. My bad. I hadn't realised that in this century the Church had become some sort of military organisation.'

'What are you talking about?' Sadkin frowned.

'Peter?'

'Mum?'

'It's time.'

'Time for what?' asked Colonel Sadkin, Father of the Chapel and leader of the military group who were, he was amazed – and a little annoyed – to see, lying unconscious on the ground. The Talpidian digger was down, too, and of Professor Jaanson there was no sign. 'What is going on?'

Peter held up a small black box with a switch on it. 'Invention of mine,' he said. 'Go into a potentially hostile situation, or one where you are hopelessly outnumbered. Shake everyone's hand, hug them even, and touch each person's skin somewhere.' In his other hand he held a small quantity of what looked like contact lenses made of rice paper. 'So light, you never know one's being attached, held there by sweat, like magnets. Then I press this switch and everyone falls asleep, painlessly, effortlessly. No bangs, no flashes, just five or six hours' refreshing sleep.'

'You'll thank me for it eventually. It really is a good deep sleep,' Bernice added.

Sadkin looked at his hand, where he'd shook Bernice's.

'You bi—' And he was down in the mud, snoring slightly.

'Bless,' said Bernice pocketing her own little black box.

Jack and Ruth re-joined them. 'Everyone accounted for except the stupid Professor,' Jack reported.

'We need to access the time portal.'

'Which is inside the pyramid, right?'

'Fundamentally, yes.' Bernice held out the rock she had been given back on Legion. 'Hopefully this'll "open sesame" and nothing else will go wrong.'

The others looked at her.

'What?'

Ruth took Benny's hand (carefully throwing away Peter's patented knock-out patches, otherwise things could have got pretty embarrassing rather quickly). 'Benny. We love you, we really do.'

'But?'

'But when was the last time we ever did anything that didn't at some point go slightly wrong?'

'Majorly wrong,' added Jack unhelpfully.

'It does happen a lot,' conceded Peter.

Bernice looked at her son in mock outrage. 'Even my own flesh and blood has no faith.'

'I'd have more faith if the person who sent us here hadn't been you.'

'A future you,' Jack reminded her.

'And if,' Ruth said, 'a future you is in so much trouble that the only solution is to go back in time to ask for help from you…' She shrugged. 'But we love you. Really. We do.'

Bernice shrugged. 'I'm not going to tell you about the

strange blue woman and the stranger fat man, then. See how you like that when we bump into them and you're not prepared. Yeah. That.'

Ruth and Jack just looked at Bernice quizzically, but Peter was back on the alert, scouring the ridges and boulders for movement made by the duo he'd spotted earlier. He pointed across the way; it was possible to see the blue-skinned female through the ice and rain. Then the fat guy came into view a few paces behind her, obviously not built for this terrain.

Peter was off in a second, expertly tracking them, moving across the plains, behind rocks, doing everything he needed to catch up with his prey without alerting them to his presence.

Bernice looked at Ruth and Jack. 'We ought to go after him.'

'What about the grumpy Professor?' Ruth asked.

'She's right beside you,' Jack giggled and nudged Ruth. She gave him a look best described as 'withering' and shook her head slowly.

But Bernice was beyond jokes now. It was time to get moving, to get serious and do what they needed to do. She was already heading off after Peter, carefully treading only in his footprints, knowing that this was the safest route.

She eventually found him crouched behind a boulder, about thirty yards from the big door in the pyramid. She gave him a questioning look and he nodded, suggesting it was OK for her to take a look.

As she did so, Ruth and Jack arrived, in utter silence,

all joking aside and working as the well-oiled machine Bernice had trained them all to be.

She felt a moment of pride. Her family. She had brought them together and made them a team.

She stared over the boulder and sure enough, the blue woman and the fat man were standing there. Then stupid Professor Jaanson arrived. She listened to him.

'About time! The Headless Monks said they'd send the best. I assume that's you.'

The fat man grunted, so the blue woman spoke. 'I'm Kik the Assassin. This is Cyrrus Globb. You must be Jaanson Horace.'

'Other way around,' he stammered, clearly in awe of Kik the Assassin. Or in fear, Bernice wasn't quite sure. 'Professor Horace Jaanson,' he corrected her. 'And behind that door is my life's work. The Monks want to understand it, I want to experience it.'

'Why?'

'Because it's a time portal. The secrets of the universe will be mine. To activate it is a lodestone, a physical key if you like. Throughout history, it had had so many names – the Locke, the Stone of Destiny, the Glamour, the Rock of Ages, whatever. But that stone exists, so legend tells, in a million places at once because of where it is positioned at the apex of the portal. If we take it, we can sell it.' He turned to Globb. 'You, I assume are a conman, a thief and a blackguard, yes?'

Globb opened his mouth, as if to protest, then shrugged. 'Pretty much. I'm the best.'

'So good you ended up in a Stormcage,' Jaanson snapped. 'I'm not impressed, but the Monks obviously were. So your job is to take the lodestone, the Glamour, and sell it, many times over, on the quiet, to every library, private collector, museum and idiot academician the universe over. Because you will actually have physical but worthless copies – visual echoes, if you like, from the time portal. I have studied this for years; my entire family before me, too. We all understand how the Ancients of the Universe built this and that they left it for someone with vision to exploit now they've passed on.'

Globb frowned. 'What if the one in there is actually one of these solid but worthless copies?' It wasn't an unreasonable question, but Jaanson was irritated by it.

'Then according to legend, we actually use that and it takes us to the original Glamour – and I study that while you flog off the others. It's very simple.'

Kik the Assassin exchanged a look with Cyrrus Globb, but the human shrugged. 'Yeah, OK, he's a loony but we're here to do a job and if he's right, we could be billionaires by next week.' Globb offered a hand to the Professor to shake. 'We have a deal.'

Jaanson didn't return the gesture. 'We're not friends, Mister Globb, purely expedient to one another's needs. Let's not get carried away.'

With a laugh, Kik the Assassin addressed the human professor. 'I like your spirit, human. My job is to protect you both and get Cyrrus here back to his cell so he can be pardoned. Well, we both can be. I'll make sure you get this

Glamour of yours. How do we get in?'

Before Jaanson could answer, Kik the Assassin's eyes flicked and Bernice realised with a chill they made direct contact with hers.

Neither of the humans was aware of what Kik the Assassin had seen, but she locked gazes with Bernice, not blinking. And after a few seconds she looked away, a massive grin on her face. 'Oh, this is going to be soooo much fun!' she shouted.

Globb and Jaanson looked at her strangely, wondering why she was being loud.

'Apologies,' she purred. 'I'm just making the most of my freedom.' She looked back at Bernice, again just slyly enough the others didn't notice. 'I love a challenge.'

And Bernice moved back to the others, holding Peter's arm.

'She saw me,' Bernice whispered.

'Why isn't she telling the others?'

Bernice shrugged. 'I can't read her as well as the humans, but my guess – she's looking for something to do that is more than guarding Globb and Jaanson's Glamour. A challenge.'

Ruth frowned. 'And we're a challenge?'

'I am. Not sure she knows you guys are here. That might work in our favour. I need to go in with them. Once we're inside, follow.' She looked at Ruth and Jack. 'This is dangerous – I doubt she's called Kik the Assassin because she's cute to babies and cuddles kittens. Do exactly what Peter says at all times.'

'We could just stay outside,' Jack suggested. 'You know what I'm like!'

Bernice shrugged again. 'Something else I didn't tell you. All four of us are trapped in that time eddy-bubble-catastrophe-thing in there. So we all need to be in there to break our future selves out of it.'

Ruth and Jack stared open-mouthed. 'And you kept that from us because?' Ruth asked.

Bernice smiled apologetically. 'It never came up.'

'Peter?' Jack turned to the teenager. 'You knew?'

'Nope,' he said. 'But I guessed.'

'How?'

'By using my brain. Mum goes on lots of missions alone. Why bring us when it's about time travel unless we're involved. Made sense.'

'Thanks, darling,' Bernice said.

'Oh, don't get me wrong, Mum. I think you're daft for not actually telling us, but that's life.' Peter smiled back at her, just baring his fangs enough. 'Don't mess it up, Mum, and we'll have your back.'

Bernice nodded and moved out.

Bernice moved carefully across the slippery surface, from boulder to boulder, trying to stay hidden. Yes, Kik the Assassin knew she was around, but if she could come from a different place it might cut through the blue woman's confidence or something.

Or probably not.

At one point, Bernice flopped down behind a large

boulder, unable to see either where she was going or where she had been. And wondered, not for the first time, if she was getting a bit old for all this.

When she had first met the Doctor, she had been significantly younger. Sig. Nif. I. Cantly. She'd had no ties to anything or anyone; she was starting out her life as a professor, as a teacher to students. She had discovered the Doctor and his friend Ace on a cemetery world called Heaven, where they had defeated a weird spore-like life form called the Hoothi, which was trying to expand itself by reanimating the corpses. Bernice had ended up travelling with the Doctor a while after that and, although she eventually moved away from the TARDIS, the two would continue to keep coming into each other's lives (quite literally in the Doctor's case, as she had seen him with more than one face). And, to some extent, Bernice envied him. He had the TARDIS, he could come and go wherever he pleased. Yes, Bernice had possessed for a short period of time a couple of Time Rings that gave her limited access to the past and future but they were unreliable and, if she was quite honest, it scared her a little to use them. It became obvious to her a few years after leaving the Doctor that her body had changed in small subtle ways that people can only notice because they are *their* bodies; they live in them from day to day; they sense things.

Bernice could already see that she aged differently to other people. She was probably in her mid-fifties now, but she looked and felt maybe fifteen years younger than that. She had an 18-year-old son, a dead husband, and at one point had had her body stolen away from her and occupied by a less-than-charming life form.

But at the back of her mind was the feeling that one day, probably soon, this was all going to come back and bite her. It was like her life was a piece of elastic; charmed, ageless, lucky and brilliant, but eventually that elastic would spring back and she'd age thirty years in a week. Whatever those Time Rings (and maybe even the TARDIS itself) had done to her would pop up and say, 'You had a good laugh, Benny, but here's where you pay the piper.' She'd once had a vision of a possible future, seeing herself dying alone on some sandy planet light years from Peter and everyone else she loved and cared about.

And yet, here she was trying to flit silently around a wet mud ball, hoping to throw herself into some weird time eddy inside a weird pyramid, and save her weird future self. Doing so would probably erase her most recent history, the future-Benny would then move forward with her life, as would Jack, Ruth and Peter, and all this would end up as some sort of daydream, a brief déjà-vu feeling.

That's time travel for you. It doesn't just mess up your body; it messes up your head.

Benny smiled to herself. 'You know what, Bernice Surprise Summerfield,' she mused to no one. 'Let's be honest, quibbles and fears aside, you wouldn't change one blasted thing about your life, would you. I mean, you loved the Doctor, you loved the TARDIS. He introduced you to Jason, to Adrian, to Guy, to Bev, to Irving, and without all of that there'd be no Peter, no Joseph, no

Dellah, no Collection, no Legion – hell, no Wolsey! In fact, no memories, no life. Imagine if you'd ended up leaving Heaven with everyone else, going back to uni; by now you'd be an old unsatisfied retired professor living in a caravan on Outer Space Mobile Home World.'

Still, all that aside, right now she'd be happier if her left hip wasn't aching, if she didn't have slight arthritis in her right knee, if the greying hairs would stay dark.

With a sigh, partially caused by pushing all those thoughts out of her mind and partially because that ruddy knee meant she wasn't as smooth getting up as she'd have liked, Bernice moved out from behind the boulder.

And found her nose being microscopically indented by the pointy end of a rapier being held by Kik the Assassin, who smiled at her.

'Nice try, saw you the moment you moved,' said Kik the Assassin. 'What do you want?'

Bernice carefully reached into her satchel and brought out the rock she'd been given earlier. 'Open sesame?' she said apologetically.

Peter Summerfield watched the blue woman lead his mother away at sword-point and drew Ruth and Jack's attention to the fact.

'We need to follow, discreetly.' He closed his eyes for a moment. 'Know what that entails, Jack?'

Jack gave him a lopsided grin. 'Oh, ye of little faith. Of course. I have survived a lot of these adventures and capers, you know.'

'Barely,' Peter growled.

Ruth tapped Peter. 'That's my husband-to-be you are dissing, young man,' she said. 'And Jack has saved your skin more times than you seem to recall right now, so less of the sarcasm.'

Peter thought about this. Nope, he really couldn't remember one moment of skin-saving by Jack, but let it go. 'Come on,' he said. 'Quietly.'

They started retracing Bernice's path around the boulders, ensuring that the blue woman's back was always to them.

'I found this skulking in the boulders,' Kik the Assassin said.

'She said earlier that she's a professor,' Jaanson said. 'But I've never heard of her.'

'I've never heard of you before today, either,' Bernice said. 'So that's really not very important. Much like you.'

'You said you knew my reputation,' Jaanson said, both affronted and clearly missing the point.

Bernice smiled at him. 'Oh dear, poor you and your ego. Look, there's the Pyramid Eternia, this is Aztec Moon and you're a pompous idiot in a tweed coat and silly hat. I've been around, Horace. I know your type.'

Jaanson drew himself up to his full height of just under five foot seven, his jowls puffing as he tried to think of some witty riposte. Instead, he just turned on his heel. 'Why not just kill her?'

'Wow, thanks, Professor,' Bernice said. 'Nice to see the

professors of the future have turned feral.'

'Shut up,' was Cyrrus Globb's contribution.

'Wait,' Jaanson said. And Bernice's eyes gleamed a little. 'Did you say "of the future"?'

'I did indeed say "of the future". Good to know the language hasn't deteriorated along with the manners.'

'Where are you from?'

'I was born in another time. Another world.'

The Professor snorted. 'Nonsense. You are one of us. You look like us, you sound like us.'

Bernice shrugged. 'I was born in the twenty-sixth century.'

Kik the Assassin gave Jaanson a glance. 'I think she's telling the truth.'

Jaanson was apoplectic – his life, his dreams were being tarnished right in front of him. 'I have spent my life searching for the answer to free movement in time and space. I don't expect to find it solved in this junkyard of a planet. Just kill her.'

'Kill me,' Bernice said quietly, with just an added dash of threat and a sprinkle of menace, 'and you'll remain trapped here, footprints in a time portal where you were not supposed to have walked.'

Professor Jaanson shrugged. 'What proof have you got to your claims?'

Bernice produced the shard of Glamour.

'And?'

Bernice shrugged. 'I don't know. I think it might gain us entry to the pyramid.' She pointed at the monolithic structure nearby. 'Fancy finding out?'

'This is nonsense,' Professor Jaanson said.

Cyrrus Globb clearly didn't have much patience. He snatched the rock out of Bernice's hand and marched over to the huge door in the pyramid. 'Now what?' he asked.

'No idea,' Bernice said truthfully. She smiled sweetly at Kik the Assassin. 'Thank you so much for dragging me into all this.'

Kik the Assassin smiled back. 'Don't worry, I trust you about as much as the human professor does. But not for the same reasons.'

'Oh?'

'Yeah, I think you're up to something. I think you probably can get us inside that Pyramid. I'm just not sure why.'

'Thanks for the vote of confidence.' Bernice then glanced at Globb. 'He really is a fool, isn't he?'

Kik the Assassin shook her head. 'Actually he's a very successful conman. I imagine he knows exactly what he's doing, but doesn't want you or the Professor to know that.'

'So why tell me?'

'Because,' the blue woman said with a little laugh that reminded Bernice of gargling with glass, 'I don't care what happens. We get in, get what the Headless Monks wanted and get out again. That way, we're free.'

Bernice thought about this. 'I see. And Jaanson?'

'Never heard of him before an hour ago. I reckon he's surplus to requirements.'

'And me?'

'We'll see. I'm not sure you're quite what you appear. That… intrigues me.'

'I like being intriguing. Usually means I'm going to stay alive a bit longer.'

Bernice focused on Globb. So he was a conman. And he needed the actual rock, this Glamour, which that shard came from, to get his freedom. Which meant it was a bargaining chip. Trouble was, she also needed the Glamour to free her future self, so it was rather important Globb didn't get it. Not so much a bargaining chip after all, more a hostage to fortune. Hmmm.

And then she walked forward, took the shard back out of his hand and held it against the doorway.

With a speed that surprised even Bernice, the door just melted away, revealing a huge dark cavern within.

Equally quickly, Globb retrieved the shard from her and pocketed it.

Deciding confidence was needed as much as a confidence trick, Bernice stepped into the darkness. Globb followed as did Kik the Assassin.

Professor Jaanson however stood on the threshold, unsure.

'You wanted to see if the time portal created by the Ancients of the Universe is home, Horace,' Bernice called out. 'Don't be chicken.'

And Professor Jaanson stepped into the gloom.

A moment later, Peter, Jack and Ruth entered through the same door, keeping quiet. Peter shifted his backpack slightly, instinctively checking just by the way it weighed that it still contained everything he suspected he might need for this mission. Ruth was checking for exits and safe routes out if it all turned bad. Jack was using his amazing eyesight to see better than the others in the dark and was focused on making sure they never lost sight of Bernice.

They moved, unspeaking, barely even acknowledging each other was there, still part of that well-oiled machine.

After a while, the darkness gave way to a distant light.

'This place is bigger on the inside than the outside,' Bernice said.

'Impossible,' said Jaanson. 'Transcendental engineering is a worthless dream and a scientific impossibility.'

Bernice sighed. The future of science really was frustrating here, if he was any example.

'Well, I can't be bothered arguing, Horace. Maybe it's all done with mirrors.'

'I imagine it is,' the Professor agreed. 'The Ancients were notoriously imaginative.'

'You're just making stuff up now, aren't you? To sound more important and educated than you actually are.'

Before Jaanson could respond, Kik the Assassin put a hand up. 'I need to check something back at the doorway.'

Globb turned open-mouthed, but the woman waved him away. 'We have a deal, Globb; it's not in my interest to abandon you. Without you getting what you want, I don't get what I want. I'll be back shortly. Bernice Summerfield will lead you forward.'

Bernice glanced back into the gloom.

Kik the Assassin leant in close so only Bernice could hear her. 'Don't worry, I won't hurt them, especially the young pup. I just need everyone together. To make sure there are no tricks.'

And she was gone faster than Bernice could think of a reply.

The light was closer now and the edges of it illuminated the sides of what was a huge chasm, created like a well in the centre (well, near as dammit) of the pyramid.

'Fascinating…' Professor Jaanson ran forward, finally shaking off his fear as he reached the edge of the chasm and looked down. 'There! There, there, there!!' He pointed excitedly at a sort of stone altar, upon which was a lump of rough stone hewn into a pyramid, to echo the big one they were within.

Bernice realised the rock was what she had the fragment of – plain, boring, white crystal running through it.

Slightly more alarming was that surrounding this altar, creating a sort of inverted funnel, like a whirlpool sucking upwards to a point, and emanating from the rock, was misty energy, still moving, like it was caught in perpetual motion.

Or, Bernice realised with dread, a time eddy.

'Who is that?' Globb harrumphed quietly.

Bernice focused, stared. 'Oh my god,' she breathed. 'There are people at the apex of that… energy.'

'Chronon energy,' Jaanson breathed.

Oh great, *now* he was acting like a scientist. And he was

probably right. Especially as Benny had already guessed who was standing there.

It had to be her. Jack. Ruth. Peter. Caught frozen, being scattered through time and sending messages and postcards and whatever to get the Doctor to find them and save them.

But of course, that wasn't going to be enough now. The vision of her future that she had spoken to was already disintegrating. It was up to her to get in there are save herself. Jump-start them.

Then maybe the Doctor would turn up, use his timey-wimey Gallifreyan whatnot to, oh who knows, probably take the Glamour away and chuck it into the heart of a supernova, make sure no one could ever try accessing the secrets of the Ancients again.

All of which might have been a plan except that suddenly sprawled beside her were Jack and Ruth, thrown some distance by Kik the Assassin.

In her other hand, she lifted Peter above her head – for the first time Bernice realised she had to be from Spyro – she had heard of the people with telescopic bones, but never seen one. But her arm was twice its original length and Peter sensibly wasn't fighting back.

'Please put my son down,' Bernice said. 'He's not great with heights.'

'We were just having a friendly chat,' Kik the Assassin said. 'It's nice to have some decent conversation for once.'

Globb gave her a look, but she just shrugged indifferently.

'And?'

Shaking his head, Globb pointed at Bernice. 'More of them?'

'Oh yes,' said Jaanson. 'She came with a gang. They took out the whole Church party.'

At any other time, that line would have made Bernice laugh. But now, she had to focus on the matter at hand. 'Jack?'

'Yes?'

How far can you jump?'

'Why don't I like where this line of questioning is going?'

'You're not meant to. All four of us need to get down there before they realise what we're up to, grab our time-locked future selves and hope the Blinovitch Limitation Effect shorts out the whole problem.'

'And if it doesn't?' Ruth asked.

'Well, usually in situations like this, two people occupying the same time, especially if they are the same time-separated people, tend to result in a big bang that takes out planets, galaxies even. We wouldn't know much about it.'

'Not particularly encouraging,' Ruth said.

'Ah,' said Benny, 'but these "duplicates" are like ghosts. They are fading from existence.'

'So,' Jack reasoned, 'we're dead either way. Now, or… whatever *then* they're from?'

'Pretty much.'

'Do we need Peter?'

'Absolutely we need Peter.'

'We don't have Peter.'

'Have faith. My adorable son will be here in a second.'

At which point Peter crashed to the ground beside them.

'How'd you do that?' Ruth asked.

'Which bit, getting free or the expert timing?'

Ruth shrugged. 'Either.'

'Expert timing – cos I'm good. Release – well, I deliberately farted.'

'You… what?'

'Dog fart,' Jack said. 'Worst smell in the universe. Good one.'

Bernice cast a look back at Kik the Assassin who was still waving the air around her face.

'Jack?'

'Yes?'

'Now.'

And Jack grabbed Ruth and Benny, who in turn grabbed her son and with the help of Jack's impressively long legs, the quartet leapt down the chasm, crashing into the time eddy.

'Grab yourselves!' Bernice yelled, but the noise just sounded like a deep, slowed-down recording, so it was indecipherable. Jack was an inch away from his future self, but Peter and Ruth were struggling.

It was like moving through treacle – and Bernice knew that her exposure to the time vortex after years of TARDISes and Time Rings and other paraphernalia would protect her slightly, but the others were utterly frozen.

Except one of them wasn't. Jack's momentum propelled him into the other Bernice, knocking into the Glamour, which crashed, in appalling slow motion to the ground.

A chip split off it and Bernice watched her future self scoop it up.

She watched as Jack then melted into his other self and Bernice realised what she needed to do.

As the future Bernice stood up, the chip of rock in her hand, Bernice shoved Ruth into Ruth. As she moved to push Peter she managed to look upwards, although it seemed to take hours or maybe days or maybe a second to turn her head.

Frozen above her were the leaping forms of Kik the Assassin and Cyrrus Globb, the latter dragging with him the terrified Horace Jaanson.

They were frozen in mid-air, because within the eye of this particular time storm, nothing moved normally.

With every effort she could muster, she pushed Peter into Peter. As with Jack and Ruth, Peter seemed to blend into his counterpart, like a photo being blurred on a computer before refocusing.

And then Bernice realised two awful things.

Instead of becoming their future selves, those future selves had taken on the clothing of her group, and the stance. And were frozen in their places.

Then one by one, Jack, Ruth, Peter and future-Bernice vanished for a few seconds, then popped back into existence, exactly where they were before.

The plan hadn't worked! Why not? Surely all she needed

to do was become her future self and everything would be OK?

And then she looked at the version of the Glamour in the centre of the altar, being touched by her future self.

And she saw the fresh gouge in the side where it had been dropped and the fragment she had been given had been chipped off.

The fragment future-Bernice no longer had! In that split second, the guys must have done all that travelling, postcard-sending and ultimately met up with Bernice back on Legion and set her on this course of action.

The fragment of the lodestone. The Glamour. Whatever.

The fragment she herself no longer had, either. Because Cyrrus Globb was holding it. And he was crashing down towards this same time eddy, and there was nothing Bernice could do.

She took a deep breath.

Either it worked or something else happened. Or they would all be time locked for the rest of eternity.

She hoped her future self had foreseen this and had a plan to sort this and avoid Globb and co, or this was going to be the fastest rescue / death plan in history.

What was it Jack had said earlier? Dead either way.

Bernice forced herself forward and became her future self.

And the time eddy changed – it got wider, larger, capturing the dropping Cyrrus Globb, Kik the Assassin and Professor Horace Jaanson it its wake.

And the time eddy vanished completely.

Then the lodestone vanished completely.

Then Bernice, Jack, Ruth and Peter vanished completely.

Then Globb, Kik the Assassin and Jaanson vanished completely.

Then the whole pyramid vanished completely.

On the red, damp surface of Aztec Moon, Colonel Sadkin groaned and pushed himself up out of the cold mud, letting the rain from above wake him.

He immediately sprang into action, yelling at his waking Clerics.

And then stopped.

The pyramid was gone, leaving a gaping hole in the ground, that got bigger as the surrounding surface of the planet cracked and fell away, into the new hole, trying to fill it.

Sadkin could do nothing else as Verger Brown, the Talpidian digger, Brother Elias and all his men one by one dropped into the hole.

And as Colonel Sadkin fell to his death, into the heart of the rapidly disintegrating planet, his last thought was of the person who had done this.

Bernice Summerfield.

6
Planet Earth

Sydney, New South Wales, Australia, Southern Hemisphere, Earth, Sol 3, Milky Way, Universe. Bit of a long address, and certainly the average postcard doesn't give anyone room to write that and put a stamp on it.

The Doctor replaced the postcard, showing the world-famous Opera House at night, in the spinner-rack. He admired the architecture and design of the Opera House, not just because Utzon's shapes created perfect acoustics, but also because it provided an excellent shadow on the Botanical Gardens side that meant he had been able to park the TARDIS in the shade with no one really noticing.

He spun the rack and selected another one. This one showed a koala in a Santa hat, holding a pennant with the Australian flag on it. WELCOME TO A SYDNEY CHRISTMAS it said, neatly avoiding the fact that koalas tended not to live in the city due to the lack of eucalyptus leaves and the general yelling and screaming and media frenzy that would result if they did. Koalas are pretty mild and shy creatures; they tended not to seek celebrity status, name their babies after soft drinks, and queue up on red carpets posing for the paparazzi. The Doctor thought koalas had pretty much got the right idea.

'I once went to a planet where the koalas were the dominant species,' he told the woman standing next to him. 'Fantastic civilisation – and certainly had the least halitosis of anywhere in the cosmos.'

The woman gave him a look and then took a step away, as if unsure that she wanted to be near a madman.

'Great conversationalists,' the Doctor added with a smile. 'Very into the arts and childcare.'

The woman tried to look busy with a couple of mugs and tea towels.

The Doctor glanced around the rest of the tourist shop. Tourists mainly (surprise, surprise), taking a souvenir home from this rather glorious city. The woman the Doctor had spoken to seemed unable to escape his gaze.

She was small – probably no more than five foot, early twenties with dark skin and long dark hair, her eyes hidden behind large sunglasses. She wore a collared black shirt and blue jeans, with a sensible pair of Chucks and had a designer handbag slung over one shoulder.

The Doctor reached towards her and tapped the bridge of her sunnies, causing them to slip slightly down her nose, so he could see her brown eyes. He grinned. 'Hullo, where are you from?'

'London,' she said in a decidedly South London accent.

The Doctor shook his head. 'No. No I don't think so.'

'Don't much care what you think, Mr Weirdo,' she

retorted, and he raised an eyebrow. This one was going to be fun, then. 'Touch me again, and I'll cripple you,' she added.

The Doctor pulled a mock 'Ooh, I'm so scared' expression and tapped her glasses again, so they actually fell off.

The small woman slapped his hand away. 'I'm warning you…' she started, but he just sighed and looked over her shoulder, scanning the shop for someone else.

'I'm sure you are,' he said dismissively, 'and I apologise if I'm annoying you, but it's your own fault.'

'How?'

'Well,' he said with a sigh, 'if you are going to visit twenty-first-century Earth, you need to do your research a little better.'

Still not actually looking at her, he pointed at her shirt. 'That's from the market in Baloo City on Jalt. The synthetics that wove together to make it simply don't exist in this solar system, and won't till the late twenty-fifth century. The bag you got, I'm guessing, from Camden Market, but not till about 2605 because that designer wasn't born till around then. And the sunglasses? They're mine, well not mine exactly, they were a gift I gave to someone once. I know that, because the slight chip in the left lens was made when we went rock-surfing on Volcana. I was more adventurous in those days. This version of me wouldn't be seen dead rock-surfing – far too dangerous.' Then he looked at her. 'So what's your name, my little non-domicile chum?'

She looked up at him, a slight smile on her face. 'I'm Ruth. And you're as good as I heard.'

'Not really, Ruth,' he said. 'You're just pretty bad at fitting in. And, if those glasses do still belong to whom I gave them to and they were loaned to you, their owner is slipping. So I think—'

The Doctor stopped. Something was pressed into the small of his back – it felt like a gun of sorts. He wasn't really in the mood to take the risk. 'So I think,' he continued, 'that a friend of yours is behind me.'

'He is,' Ruth said. 'Armed.'

'I guessed.'

'Fancy guessing what kind of gun, where it was manufactured and how I got it to Earth?' said a male voice behind him.

'Guns aren't my thing,' the Doctor said.

'Good,' said the male. He had a deep, but also soft voice. It was a voice that was probably used to getting what it wanted.

'If I promise not to make a scene, would you mind putting the gun away?' the Doctor said. 'You know, before any of the humans in here notice?' He scanned the shop – ah, perfect, over by the baseball caps area was a mirror. He could see himself and Ruth in it, and behind him, equally short, a figure in a grey hoodie, the top pulled up so high and forward that there was no chance of getting even a glimpse of the face. And the angle wasn't good enough to confirm it was a gun and not a comb or porcelain kangaroo jabbed into his back.

'Can't say I give a damn if the humans do see anything,' the gunman responded.

It was an act, the Doctor decided. The voice betrayed that. He wasn't quite as aggressive and sarcastic as he pretended to be. But probably enough that it wasn't worth calling his bluff. Yet. 'What would you like me to do?'

'There's a café along the waterfront. Meet us there in ten minutes.'

The Doctor sighed. 'We're in Darling Harbour, there's barely an establishment here that isn't a café.'

'Coffee shop,' said the male.

'Field not narrowing,' the Doctor replied. 'What's it called?'

Neither of his new 'friends' had an answer for that.

'It has green umbrellas outside,' the male said eventually. 'Ask for Jack.'

The Doctor gritted his teeth. 'Again. Darling Harbour. Sydney. Any idea how many people in any given café, even one with green umbrellas outside, will be called Jack?'

At which point, something slammed into his upper back (probably a fist) and he went flying forward, crashing into the postcard spinner, and he fell flat on his face, bringing down a display of horrible pink and glitter T-shirts as well.

Shoppers looked aghast as he tried to salvage dignity and get straight back up but realised someone had tied his shoelaces together. He staggered and fell again.

Of his assailants, there was no sign and, by the time he'd freed his feet and grudgingly apologised to the storeowners, ten minutes was nearly past. He left the shop, ignoring the looks and tuts from his fellow customers and scanned both sides of Darling Harbour.

Christmas. In the heat. It seemed wrong, the Doctor thought, that no matter where you went in the universe, Christmas was represented by red-jacketed Santas, reindeer and green pointy Christmas trees. Sydney, despite this being the height of summer, was no exception.

The waterfront was decorated as if it were a bitter New York winter, or a savage Welsh one. Inflatable, jolly, fat, heavily-swathed-in-red-clothes Santas were clustered on a barge. The lampposts were wrapped in tinsel and snowflakes, whilst giant snowmen wobbled atop many buildings and one was suspended on the fascia of the Anzac Road Bridge. It just seemed wrong, bearing in mind Sydney probably saw enough snow in an average year to fill a teaspoon.

The harbour was, as he'd said earlier, mostly a vast array of restaurants and bars and coffee shops on both sides of the water, developed in the last decade or so into one of the city's main 'must-see' areas, supplying the handful of hotels in the area that charged a premium for a 'water view'. He looked to his right. The humongous Pyrmont footbridge, to the right, the IMAX cinema and the Friendship Garden. He scanned all the storefronts, looking for one nearby that had green umbrellas.

None of them. He went right, following the curve of the harbour round to the other side, trying not to get irritated with the slow-wandering pedestrians that always seemed to materialise in front of him when he was in a hurry.

Why were there no set rules for walking? Cars had lanes. Bikes had lanes. Why not pedestrians? How much simpler the world(s) would be if pedestrians had to walk fast on the left and slower on the right. Maybe they could have a middle lane where they could drift in and stop and chat to friends. And thus stay out of his way.

Mind you, this was a schizophrenic country that had one foot still in its colonial origins as a British discovery and the other in modern, fast-paced America. It was a weird amalgam of both cultures – Darling Harbour being a prime example. It used the British spelling of 'harbour' whilst adopting American spellings for words like 'labor'. And don't even get him started on their use of the word 'thongs', which had one meaning in Australia and a wholly different one throughout the rest of the entire universe.

No wonder the people who lived there were so confused they couldn't walk around a semi-circular harbour in a straightforward orderly fashion and stay out of his way!

He was suddenly aware from the looks he was getting that this last set of thoughts had actually been said (well, OK, really rather yelled) out loud. A woman in a green bikini and her partner, a buff guy in shorts and 'thongs' (definitely not flip-flops), were standing in front of him.

'Look mate if you don't like 'Stralia, go back home, you Irish ponce.'

The Doctor stared at him and heard himself say, 'Scottish ponce, actually,' then wondered why. After all, he was Gallifreyan, it wasn't his fault that he had ended up with a particular distinctive human accent. Perhaps one day he'd get an Aussie accent (but which one, AuE, Strine or… shudder… bogan?)

He slapped the side of his head. 'Focus. I really should focus,' he said to the two Australians then marched past them as if they simply weren't annoying him any more.

He was then aware that he was being carefully watched. He checked, made sure nothing else could be interesting this stranger, but no, it was definitely him being watched. Observed might have been a better word. An indigenous male, tall, dark, dressed in a white shirt and chinos. The man smiled at the Doctor, nodded, then turned and just seemed to melt into the crowd. Weird, the Doctor decided, but not a priority because he had to find this 'Jack' person.

Focus.

Yes! There was a café-bar. He stopped. It was called the White Rabbit, and sure enough had green umbrellas outside.

The White Rabbit?

Like the place on Legion.

Or the pub on the Thames Embankment.

Or the bar on Bedrock 12.

Or…

The Doctor stood outside and stared in. It was utterly deserted. The only café place in the whole area not heaving. Indeed, bearing in mind how many people were queuing to get into the other places, it seemed weird that this was empty.

'Shimmer,' he muttered, wondering what everyone else saw this building as.

He scanned the ground. Sure enough, the Shimmer control was down to the right, near an umbrella. To anyone else, he assumed, he was walking into a closed-off shop or something.

'That's a lot of effort,' he called into the empty place. 'Why not just leave it as it really is?'

'There are a lot of buildings being done up around here,' replied someone new. 'Thought this might be more appealing.'

'There are a lot of coffee shops too,' the Doctor retorted. 'You didn't think that would be equally confusing?'

'Ah, but how many of them are called the White Rabbit?'

'Why didn't your goons just say that? Looking for the Rabbit would have been a lot easier than looking for a place with green umbrellas.'

'Because,' said Ruth who was suddenly beside him, staring angrily into the empty café, 'it wasn't called the White Rabbit when we left. Idiot.'

'I'm not an—'

'Not you,' she snapped at the Doctor. 'Him. In there.'

The small guy in the grey hoodie was now standing on the other side of the Doctor. 'Get what you deserve in this life, Ruth,' he said.

And as he stepped past the Doctor, he flicked his hoodie down and the Doctor saw him for what he was. In many respects, he was just a smallish teenaged boy, maybe 17 or 18. What marked him out as more than a bit unusual was that instead of human ears, he had ears like those on a Doberman pinscher or Rottweiler coming from close to his crown, and his nose was more of a snubby canine snout. His irises were pitch black and the Doctor caught a glimpse of some very animalistic teeth as he grimaced going forward. His hands were quite human, although very matted with downy, mottled fur and in one hand he carried a small blaster – presumably the one he'd pushed into the Doctor's back. His trousers were army combats, but wrapped around each thigh were straps with pouches and holsters. This lad was armed to the teeth and the Doctor didn't try to imagine what weaponry was under the hoodie, or concealed elsewhere.

The final surprise of the day (or so the Doctor hoped) was Jack. He emerged from the shadows, ignoring the stroppy teenager, and wandered over to hug Ruth. 'Awww Ruthie, I loves ya!' He cocked his head and winked at the Doctor. 'Wotcha.'

The Doctor recognised his species – the burning red eyes, pointed ears and chin, and the incredibly long legs with their pronounced knee-crook forward, meaning he could jump like a grasshopper and probably to quite some height. And that cheeky, devil-may-care attitude that was endemic of Kadeptians.

'Lawyer? Accountant? IT?'

'Dad's a lawyer,' Jack said. 'I got out. Borrring.'

'And here you are, on Earth, in the twenty-first century with Ruth and…' The Doctor waved towards the stroppy-but-heavily-armed teenager.

Jack leaned forward, conspiratorially. 'Oh, that's Peter. He's being a bit of a 'mare at the moment. Met someone in a club on Bacchus Five, thought this was the romance to end all romances.'

'But it wasn't,' Ruth added quietly, her voice carry slightly more empathy for Peter than Jack's. 'He was put off by Peter's human-Killoran physiology.'

'Dog-ears,' Peter called over, pointing at his large ears. 'Can hear everything.'

'See what I mean? Can't hide anything you say from old aerial ears over there.'

'Seriously, I have a gun, not afraid to use it!'

'You've had twelve months to shoot me, Petey,' Jack called back. 'Somehow I don't think you're going to do it now.' Jack turned back to the Doctor. 'Loves me really.'

'Someone has to,' Ruth said.

'Hey, don't say that to the man who put a ring on your finger.'

Jack smiled, and the Doctor found himself smiling too at Jack's charm. Then remembered this was also a trick of everyone on Kadept. (This was why they made good lawyers and accountants and IT techs – they could tell you anything and you'd believe it.)

Ruth held her hand up. 'See this ring? Oh no, wait, there is no ring because someone had to pawn it to pay a debt off.'

Jack beeped her nose. 'And I'll buy you a new one. Probably from here. Be worth a fortune back home – it'll be an antique there!'

Ruth sighed. 'Sorry about Jack.'

'You're the one marrying him,' the Doctor said. 'He's

your problem, not mine. I just want to know why you went to such a charade to bring me here.'

'That's the boss,' Jack said. 'Said to reel you in, like a fish on a hook; like a donkey seeking a carrot; like a moth looking for a flame; like a—'

'OK, I get it. A simple "Hi, we're from the twenty-seventh century, fancy a pot of tea' would have had the same effect.'

'Ahh,' Jack said. 'But would that have been as much fun? Besides, we're working to a countdown here.'

And with a rather overblown flourish, he whipped a traditional stopwatch from a pocket and held it up. It may have looked trad, but the face was a digital timer counting down. 'Five, four, three, two, one. And: cue!'

The Doctor looked around, waiting for something to happen. To their credit, so did Jack, Ruth and Peter.

But nothing did happen.

They all looked at each other for a few seconds. Jack shrugged slowly.

And then the screaming outside started.

Jack turned to Ruth. 'Told you it was a cheap one.' He looked at the Doctor. 'Bet Time Lords have clocks that work.'

The Doctor wasn't sure whether the revelation they knew where he was from or the screaming from the people in Darling Harbour was more important at that moment, but frankly screaming people was more likely to need sorting, and rushing out of the empty café at least got him away from the three mad people.

As he ran, he scooped up the Shimmer and switched it off. The café vanished and was replaced by a small disused shop, with a poster for a circus from six months earlier pasted to a cracked glass door.

'Spoilsport,' Ruth muttered and followed him. So did Jack and Peter, who pulled his hoodie back up, just in case anyone saw him. Jack seemed less fussed about his appearance, although at a glance, he just seemed like someone moderately tall who could run fast, so most Australians wouldn't notice him.

The Doctor was scanning the surroundings. Where was the screaming coming from?

All around.

OK, where had it started?

The biggest group of running people seemed to be coming from within the walled Chinese Friendship Garden so, moving against the hordes of running humans, the Doctor tried to push his way into the direction they were coming.

A hand gripped his and pulled him forward.

The Doctor tried to see the face of his gripper, but every time he took his eye off where they were going, someone careered into him, spinning him. All the time, the hold on his hand got tighter. They weren't going to let go.

So he stopped. Dead.

The woman holding him was yanked back towards him, and he caught her expertly.

As her head fell back against his chest, deep-blue eyes looked up from under a mop of dark hair, and a beautiful bright grin that, the Doctor had to admit, could light up a dark room, made him relax.

'You,' he said.

'Me,' she said.

'Of course,' he said. 'I just met your son. He's grown up fast.'

'Killoran DNA,' she said. 'Does that to you. Last time I saw you, you were a bit younger and a bit shorter. But still Scottish. Again. Time travel is very confusing, you know.'

He pulled the woman upright. She was also wearing a black shirt and jeans, similar to Ruth's outfit.

'Tell me about them?'

'Who?'

'Your "team".'

'Well, Peter, as you know, is my son. He's also my expert in bangs and flashes – if it needs shooting, knocking out or blowing up, he's who I trust to do it efficiently, cleanly and practically.' She then looked to where Ruth was easing her way through the crowd, effortlessly and sensibly, weaving and ducking where necessary. 'Ruth, I trust with my life. She has good instincts, she's a thinker and can usually see the solution to a problem just by walking into a room and having it explained to her when the rest of us have been discussing it for hours and getting nowhere.'

'And him?'

'Jack? Oh Jack's… I'm really not quite sure what Jack's for, but he's sweet, funny and makes us all laugh. He's also clumsy, often speaks without thinking first and has a habit of being blunt to the point of rudeness, but we never care, because we're too busy laughing. He can also jump pretty far.'

As the crowd thinned out around them, she smiled at him again. 'So… you got the Scots accent back, from… well, from your perspective anyway, from a few more bodies ago. Less Highlander, more Glaswegian I reckon.'

The Doctor sighed. 'Always one for the minutiae, never the bigger picture.'

'Not fair,' she said. 'I'm very much a "bigger picture" woman. I'm here because of the pyramid in the harbour.'

The Doctor glanced back. 'No pyramid.'

'Not here, not Darling Harbour. I mean the big one, with the bridge and that delightful opera house, and all the ocean liners.'

'There's no pyramid there, either. I think I might have noticed.'

'Ah,' she said. 'It hasn't arrived yet. But it will. That's why they're here.'

'Who?'

'Bigger picture, Doctor.' And she pointed towards the Peace Gardens.

Standing, looking like they were trying to acclimatise themselves, were three figures that definitely did not look like they belonged on twenty-first-century Earth.

The Doctor sighed. 'It's always trouble when you're around, isn't it?'

She laughed. 'Oh Doctor, you know me, Professor Bernice Summerfield, here to save the world.'

At which point, the three newcomers noticed the fact

that, unlike everyone else, the Doctor and Bernice weren't running away.

'You!' one of them said.

'They seem to know you,' the Doctor observed.

'Everyone loves Bernice,' she replied, and brought a stopwatch out of her pocket, like the one Jack had earlier, the Doctor noted. It also had a timer. It was three seconds away from something.

Bernice smiled.

And then the really, *really* big noise, mixed with screams, yells, car horns, ship horns and a lot of water happened.

Bearing in mind how far away Sydney Harbour actually was, the Doctor was impressed that they could hear it all from where they were.

Which also suggested that 'it' was very big.

He and Bernice turned to follow the eye line of the alien with the gun, whose eyes had widened at the noise.

And in the distance, the tip of something triangular was now part of the Sydney skyline, just to the right of where the Harbour Bridge should be.

'Told you,' Bernice whispered. 'Pyramid. In Sydney Harbour. Just outside Circular Quay. Goddess, I'm good at this.'

The Doctor was still keeping half an eye on the newcomers. The massive human who looked like his heart should give out at any moment carrying that amount of weight jabbed his pudgy finger towards the Doctor.

'And who is this?' he boomed with a voice that sounded like it was swallowing jelly. Or maybe gelignite.

'This is the leader of this little entourage, this group, this gang. That, Cyrrus Globb, is the man wanted on every civilised world for cons and grifts of the highest order. This is the leader of us all, this is the legendary brains of my outfit – meet Doc.'

And the Doctor realised, not for the first time, but certainly the first time this week, that whatever was going on, he was not only completely in the dark, but also in way above his head.

He leaned slightly in towards Bernice and muttered, so this Globb person couldn't hear: 'Benny Summerfield, I want you to know just how much I hate you right now.'

7

Criminals in the Capitol

Senior Sergeant Rhodes had seen a lot in his career. Everything from hoons trying to bungee jump from the Sydney Harbour Bridge to uptight and over-privileged politicos demanding the best seats at the St George Open Air cinema despite not having bought tickets. He'd dealt with speeding cars full of criminals, he'd dealt with irate parents, and once he'd even had to ask a famous pop star not to do an impromptu free gig in the middle of Pitt Street.

But he doubted that he'd ever dealt with anything quite so weird as a massive pyramid just appearing in the harbour, right in front of the bridge on the Circular Quay side. Apart from the shipping it was blocking, and the choppy waters that were playing havoc with the ferries and tourist boats, the biggest problem was the car shunts that had occurred on the bridge when people got, understandably distracted. Luckily, his colleagues in the Ambulance Service hadn't reported any major injuries.

But all the triple-zero services were reporting a great deal of calls, and it was hardly surprising. Senior Sergeant

Rhodes was standing at the Hickson Road Reserve, getting the best view of what was either a massive publicity stunt for a movie that no one had bothered telling the authorities about, or was some weird installation from the Museum of Contemporary Art just behind him.

Either way, it shouldn't be in the water. Shouldn't even be in Sydney without the proper authorisation.

Thing was, the more he looked at it – and he was about as close as you could get without actually swimming to it, it didn't look faked. The stonework, for all its weird carved shapes and design, looked… heavy. Looked real. Which it couldn't be because if it was, it would weigh tonnes and there was no way something that big and heavy got moved through the city and dumped without anyone seeing it.

'It just appeared,' said a man.

The senior sergeant looked at him. Dirty, dishevelled, quite smelly, with a small ratty-looking dog on a piece of string.

'Morning Jarhead,' Rhodes said to the old wino. 'When did it get put there?'

'Seriously, man,' 'Jarhead' Jared Kelly said. 'I watched it just… appear. One minute it wasn't there, the next, bang, there it was. Kally here saw it too, didn't you, darl?'

Kally the dog barked her agreement. Or just barked. Kally barked a lot. Usually when one of Rhodes's men arrested 'Jarhead' for being drunk. Which was a pretty regular thing.

That would certainly tie in with why everyone was screaming and shouting earlier, the Senior Sergeant reckoned, but it still didn't explain how the thing got there. And 'Jarhead' was hardly the most reliable of witnesses. Last time he was brought in, he was talking about little green men from Mars trying to dismantle the Harbour Bridge, so it was safest to take everything he said with a pinch of salt.

And whilst it absolutely didn't tell the policeman exactly how it got there, more significantly, it offered up no clues as to why it was there. Or who put it there.

It was going to be a long day.

The Doctor had led his little group down to Circular Quay, where they did their best to melt into the gathered crowds who, having got over their initial shock and fear, were now for the most part lined up along the side of the Opera House, or on Platform 2 of Circular Quay station, getting good selfies of themselves with the pyramid in the background.

'So what is it?' they heard one bloke ask.

'Good question,' the Doctor muttered, brought out his own smartphone and took a photo.

'You want me to get one of you with it?' asked Ruth sweetly.

The Doctor just gave her a look and sent the photo to Keri back on Legion, with the accompanying message: Recognise this?

Bernice leaned in, so Cyrrus Globb, Kik the Assassin and Horace Jaanson couldn't hear. 'That's our mission, Boss,' she said.

'Mission?'

'Yup, mission. We have to get inside it. To do that we have to track down the original lodestone that operates it. To do that, we have to find out where it first arrived on Earth and bring it back here, without actually touching it.'

'Oh, I am so going to regret this: and why, dear Benny, should we not touch it?'

'Well, it's just a guess, but touching it is what zapped me, Peter, Ruth and Jack here. Then, a few twisted timelines later, it deposited Globb and co. And then, a few more twisted timelines later, it actually deposited the pyramid. Now, I'm no expert – and you have no idea how hard it is for me to say that out loud – but if I was at the epicentre and got zapped here, they other were further away and wound up here a few days later, closely followed by the pyramid, it suggests to me that things are being sent here sequentially.'

'And that's not good because?'

'Well, because next up may well be some pretty pissed off soldiers from a place called Aztec Moon, who seem to work for a church.'

'The Church of the Papal Mainframe?'

'That's them, Boss!'

'What were you doing in the fifty-first century? How did you time travel?'

'Fragment of lodestone, given to me by my future self who was trapped in a time eddy at the self-same epicentre I mentioned earlier. Not sure if I'm her, she's me or we've sorted of blended into one thing now, that's interesting, I hadn't stopped to think about that… Anyway, long story short, chip of lodestone had enough oomph to draw me and the others to our future selves but not enough to protect us from the master stone as it were.'

'Except that it wasn't, was it?'

'Wasn't what?'

'The master lodestone. It was just a time echo that had been locked in place while waiting for the real lodestone, which is presumably here. So yes, we need to get the real lodestone inside the pyramid, lock it into place and send everything back to the fifty-first century before the universe explodes.'

Bernice frowned. 'Not sure I like this new melodramatic you. The universe is hardly going to explode because someone dumped a pyramid here. I mean Earth, yes. Because I imagine Aztec Moon will eventually be transported here as well, and two planets on top of one another can't be good for Earth. Or Mars. Or the sun. But the whole universe?'

'Aztec Moon, yes? The world you were on? And that's Professor Horace Jaanson, right? He's smaller than I remember from the pictures, but I know his work.'

'Did you know he's a prat?'

'Everyone knows he's a prat.'

'Oh good.' Bernice smiled. 'So long as it's not just me that thinks it.'

'So Aztec Moon plus Jaanson plus a lodestone most commonly referred to as the Glamour. You know it's a word from the time of the Great Old Ones? Though whether this is actually the legendary Glamour, I rather doubt. There again it could be. Or maybe the term has been applied to various powerful objects over the years, in which case—'

'Doctor?'

'Yes?'

'Stay on the point?'

He nodded. Good call. 'So, now we have a pyramid that is in Sydney rather than where it ought to be. And that suggests one thing to me.'

'Which is?'

'The Ancients of the Universe.'

Bernice winked. 'Got it in one, Boss.'

'Stop calling me "Boss". Why did you tell Globb I was your team's leader?'

Bernice indicated Globb with her head. 'He's apparently some great conman, recently in prison; the turquoise lady is a Spyro weaponista called Kik the Assassin. Yes, that's really her name, not a description. She's also rather taken with my son. Hence us getting a bit more information before we all got zapped back here.'

'I repeat, why did you tell him—'

'Because,' Bernice interrupted, 'I want him to think we're all on the same side.' She suddenly adopted a very bad London accent. 'Doin' a grift, mate, innit? Know wot I mean, guv?'

The Doctor just stared at her, closed his eyes, took a deep breath, opened them again and looked at her without smiling. 'I liked you in the twenty-seventh century,' he said. 'I feel safe with you in the twenty-seventh century. I don't go to the twenty-seventh century any more.'

Bernice just beeped his nose. 'You miss me. Now, tell me how this pyramid is going to blow up the universe.'

'Oh that's simple,' he said, carefully wiping the end of his nose where Bernice had beeped him. 'The Ancients of the Universe manipulated all of time and space for their own ends, then vanished, leaving their famous Pyramid Eternia to be stayed away from. The youngest time tot on Gallifrey learnt that. Because what you are referring to as a lodestone, what others call the Glamour, or the Stone of Destiny, is an incredibly powerful key. And what do keys do?'

'Lock things up? Leaving them safe?'

'Or?'

'Unlock things. Leaving them unsafe.'

'Especially if you remove the key. So imagine that, by taking that key away, inch by inch or rather microsecond by microsecond, what you were opening was a portal to all of space and time. When it comes crashing through, it reverberates throughout all of space and time.'

'And?'

'And, Professor, as each bit of space and time touches another piece of space and time it wasn't supposed to touch, they annihilate one another. And in the space of about three heartbeats, past, present and future are nullified. The Big Bang never happened, and yet at the same time it happens in every microsecond like a chain reaction. The universe is, what's the phrase I was looking for? Oh yes, gone.'

'Then we need to stop Globb or Jaanson or whoever getting into the pyramid and stealing your key…' Bernice realised. 'Which of course we already did, but it wasn't the real key, it was a temporal echo, and the real key is here and the Pyramid Eternia has come back looking for the key and we need to place the real key in the place of the echo key and stop the universe going bang.'

'Spot on.'

'Why here? Why now? I mean what's so special about the key in 2015?'

The Doctor shrugged. 'Haven't the foggiest.'

'Well then you're a fat lot of good,' Bernice said. 'We need to find someone who does know.' She looked at Professor Horace Jaanson.

'If he knew,' the Doctor said, 'he'd already have it in his hands. But what Horace Jaanson actually knows about anything can be written on the back of a postage stamp. We need access to the repository of all knowledge.'

'The Matrix on Gallifrey?'

The Doctor opened his mouth to speak, but didn't.

Bernice reached out, took his hand. 'I'm sorry. What did I say?'

'Gallifrey is…' The Doctor tried to find the right word. 'Missing.'

Bernice clearly wanted to ask a thousand questions about that statement but let it go, just squeezed his hand a bit tighter, unsure if she was comforting him or herself at that moment. Bernice was immediately focused, all banter aside as she started making a plan.

'We need to find out why the Pyramid Eternia has drawn us all here, then. I would assume because the Glamour, key, whatever, is here somewhere and for some reason isn't here later than this era. I mean, I don't know how exact pyramids are when traveling through space and time, but my guess would be that it isn't so much today that's important as this general period.'

The Doctor nodded. 'If time is in a state of flux, getting the key back inside the pyramid is urgent but doesn't have to be done in the next five minutes. That said... every minute we do delay might be doing terrible things to the Web of Time.'

'The joy being, if it can be said to be a joy, that the universe, and us, won't be aware of it until the fireworks start. Teeny tiny tweaks and changes the fabric of the universe can deal with.'

She stopped and looked at the Doctor and suddenly they both laughed. 'This is just like old times, Benny. You and I, facing impossible odds and coming up with more metaphors and synonyms than actual solutions.'

'I know,' she said. 'I missed it. I missed you. Even this you,' she said waving her hand towards the man whose mind she knew but whose face was still a stranger.

'I need to make a phone call,' the Doctor said. 'Care to walk with me?'

Bernice leaned back towards her son. 'Peter, we'll be back in a few minutes. Don't let Globb and co out of our sight for a second.'

Peter nodded. 'I'm all eyes and ears.'

She squeezed his arm. 'Love you.'

'Go,' he said. 'Now. Or I'll scream that a strange old woman is professing her weird affection for me.'

Shaking her head, Bernice slipped away after the Doctor. He was tapping his smartphone.

'Who are you calling?'

The Doctor held up a finger to shush her as he waited for a connection and a beat later, he spoke.

'It's me.' Beat. 'Well who do you think "me" is?' Beat. 'The person who gave you the phone so he could call you and not get messed around.' Beat. 'Then he sighed. 'Putting you on speakerphone.'

He looked at the fascia of the phone, his finger hovering, looking for something to tap. After a ridiculous amount of time and an equally ridiculous lack of movement, Bernice snatched the phone and with two taps, had the speakerphone activated.

She could immediately hear badly piped music and a lot of yelling. That sounded like… the White Rabbit. On Legion. Her home. Well, obviously the bar wasn't her home but she certainly spent a lot of time in it, mainly because it was run by her good friend Irv—

Then a voice broke her line of thought.

'Have you done it yet, you ridiculous man? Can I speak yet, yeah?'

Bernice stared open-mouthed, shot the Doctor a look then stared at the phone.

'Keri? Ker'a'nol? What the hell are you doing on Legion?'

'Who the hell is – oh. Oh, Benny, is that you, yeah?'

'Of course it's me, who else is stupid enough to get stuck on primitive Earth with him?'

'Was it you? The postcards? All that stuff that dragged me here? To this dead-end part of the universe?'

'Yeah. Well no. Well, sort of. It was future-me.'

'Well, next time you see future-you, slap her for me. In the meantime, when I next see you-you, I'm slapping you in case I don't get a chance to slap future-you.'

'Why. Are. You. There?'

'I. Don't. Know. You dragged me here.'

'Why did I do that? Rather, why will I do that?'

'I. Don't. Know! How many times do I have to say that? Where's the Doctor?'

'I'm here.' The Doctor leaned towards the phone, trying to take it from Bernice's hand, but she kept moving away, because she wasn't going to let go.

'And how is he calling you in the twenty-seventh century from here in the twenty-first?'

'Is that where you are? Oh, how exciting.'

'It's not exciting, it's alarming.'

'I thought you liked the twenty-first century,' the Doctor said.

Bernice shot him a look. 'I love it. Just not when it and the whole universe is in danger of becoming part of the Big Bang generation, permanently!'

'I thought you loved it, too,' Keri said. 'So what are you calling me for, Benny? Other than to apologise for all this, I hope.'

Bernice wasn't sure whether to throw the phone away.

Instead she opted to pass it back to him, muttering, 'So, Keri gets one of your universal roaming phones. I travelled with you in the TARDIS for ages. I introduced you to Keri. I made sure your friends stopped wanting to shoot you. Do I get a phone?'

'No,' Keri interrupted, 'I got it instead.'

'He has more than one phone,' Bernice snapped. 'And lots of people he gives them to. Except me, it seems.'

'Moving on,' the Doctor said, finally able to prise the phone from Bernice's hand, 'Keri, I need you to spring into action.'

'What do you need?'

'Everything you can find out about the world known as Aztec Moon and a man called Horace Jaanson who I recall being an expert on the Pyramid Eternia – which was the photo I sent you, by the way.'

'Narrow the field, Doctor, those are very big fields.'

'The key, then. Try, Glamour. Rock of Ages. Stone of Destiny. Lodestone. Anything.'

'All right, all right,' snapped Keri. 'God, Benny, this one's more impatient than any of the others, yeah?'

'And grumpier.'

'I noticed that,' Keri agreed.

'The universe is about to end, and you're nattering rather than researching,' the Doctor said. 'I'm entitled to be grumpy.'

'Yeah but don't take it out on us,' Keri said. 'Benny has got her work cut out trying to stop you annoying and insulting people.'

'Yeah,' Benny echoed. 'And Keri has her work cut out trying to do this research while you're nagging at her.'

The Doctor sighed. 'One minute you're at one another's throats…'

'OK,' Keri said. 'So all that I can find here is that at some point in the future – this phone's GalWiki search function is truly multidimensional, that's cool. Can I keep it, Doctor, yeah?'

'Focus.'

'Oh right, yeah. So in the future, as far as I can tell, somewhere around 5064, the world called Aztec Moon explodes for unknown reasons. The Pyramid Eternia is assumed lost for ever, but some kind of causal nexus opens up and huge shards of the planet vanish into it and no one knows where they went because even by then, the average schmuck doesn't have access to space-time vortexes. End of.'

'OK,' Bernice said. 'So that ties into what we already guessed. So let's make an assumption here, because that's pretty much all we have time for. This causal nexus thing shoots rocks at Earth, including the Glamour, its lodestone. It lands here somewhere, in 2015 and that's why the Pyramid Eternia is here – it wasn't destroyed on Aztec Moon, it came here.'

'All good,' Keri said, 'except there are absolutely no reports of anything as major as that hitting Earth in 2015.'

'I could have told you that,' the Doctor said. 'We'd know about it historically. Truth is, 2015 is a pretty uninteresting year, universally speaking.'

Bernice nodded. 'OK, so it didn't arrive here, it arrived in the past.'

'Or the future, yeah?' Keri suggested.

'If it was in the future, the Pyramid Eternia would have dragged us to there. I reckon it has to be in the past.'

The Doctor thought about this. 'Earth isn't exactly free from meteor showers over its history – most go unrecorded.'

Bernice nodded. 'Can't be Tunguska – you and I both know what that was about.'

'Possibly Qingyang,' the Doctor said. He clicked his fingers. 'Murchison, that was in Australia!'

'Too recent,' Keri reported over the phone. 'We know what came from that, it's well reported. Oh, hang on, yeah.'

'Well?'

'Patience. Grumpy and impatient. I liked the other one with a Scots accent far better,' Keri said.

'I still do,' said Bernice. 'In fact, just the other week I said to h—' And she stopped. 'No, never mind.'

The Doctor took another one of those deep breaths he was taking a lot of recently and tried to get everyone back on topic.

'You said it's known as the Glamour, right?' asked Keri.

'Yeah,' said Bernice, before getting a stern look from the Doctor.

'Why?' he asked.

'Explorer in Australia, about a hundred years back, found something he referred to as the Glamour.'

'We could go back in time and grab it before he does,' Bernice suggested, but the Doctor shook his head.

'No, that'll just cause another temporal echo. We have to know where to find it here.'

'We don't actually know what we're looking for,' Bernice reminded him. 'I mean I have a chip of it and saw it in a blurry time eddy kind of thing, but put me in a room of moon rocks and I can't guarantee I could pick it out.'

'There's another problem,' Keri said quietly. 'The reference just vanished from GalWiki.'

'What does that mean?' Bernice asked.

'It means,' the Doctor said seriously, 'that time has already started changing.' He leaned in closer to the hone. 'Keri, I need you to tell me whatever you can find about this explorer, who he was and what connections he has to 2015. Benny and I will have to nip back and make sure he does what history needs him to, if you can recall what GalWiki said before it changed.'

'And if we don't?'

The Doctor grimaced. 'Then the destruction of the universe will take a massive step closer to now because time is already unravelling. That Pyramid is going to take the universe out like you blowing out a candle. Very, very soon.'

Peter Summerfield was looking for his mother, trying not to draw Jaanson or Globb's attention whilst he did so, hoping that they were still swept up by the sight of the Pyramid Eternia standing exactly where it shouldn't be.

There was also the possibility they were taken in a bit by just how nice Sydney looked in the sunshine. He was, and wished he could get his hoodie off, but suspected the humans of 2015 weren't quite ready for his appearance.

'Where is she?'

Peter swung around.

Kik the Assassin was standing there, ignoring the looks of the locals who really weren't that used to turquoise humans. Maybe they thought she was part of whatever exhibition / film premiere most people were putting this event down to.

'Who? Ruth – probably inside, trying to stop Jack accidentally breaking things. He does that a lot.'

'Your mother, puplet. Where is she and her leader, Doc?'

Resisting the urge to point out how much his mum would not have appreciated that delineation, he just shrugged. 'She was here a second ago. Maybe they went to the back of the building for a better look?'

Kik the Assassin smiled. 'You are a good liar, Peter. A good soldier, too. In another life, we could be coupled, mate and have amazing offspring. We should do that when this is over.'

Peter smiled. 'You're not my type, lady – and I think I'd be pretty disappointing as a result.'

Kik the Assassin nodded. 'How parochial and typically human.' She turned and walked away.

Which troubled Peter. Why was she no longer wondering where his mum and the Doctor had got to? It meant either she was playing some other game, or she already knew. And that meant Kik the Assassin knew more than Peter did, which was more troubling.

One of the advantages that Peter had over other teenagers was that his Killoran heritage meant that, like most canine species, his hearing was very good, way better than an average human's. So when the TARDIS dematerialisation sound occurred, he heard it.

He sighed. More covering up to do while the Doctor took his mum to God knows where…

8
All She Wants Is

It was 22 December 1934, and Tomas G. Schneidter was
not having a great day. Truth was, he wasn't even having
a good one.

For a start, it was raining. All the time he had spent
aboard the ship that had brought him here, all he heard
from the British and Americans aboard was 'Oh, you're
gonna love Australia, it's sunshine all the way' and 'I say,
Australia's a jolly marvellous place, awfully warm and
green.' One can never understand why, when Captain
Cook arrived, he didn't just send the convicts back to
small, dirty, cold Britain and move the upper classes to
Australia instead, what?' But no one had pointed out that
when it rains in New South Wales, it really rains. And in
the famous Blue Mountains, the rain runs down into all the
gullies and valleys, turning everything into quite a mess of
mud and sludge with very little cover. The trees seemed to
have evolved leaves that, rather than keeping the rain off
you, actually bent down at an angle guaranteed to ensure
the water poured down the back of your collar.

The other reason his day wasn't turning out the way he had anticipated was the presence of his wife. He loved his wife. Absolutely. No, really, he did. After all, she was charming, attractive, witty, elegant and above all incredibly rich. Which was great for parties, fundraising events and getting into the best restaurants in Dachau and Munich.

She was also demanding, spoiled, and utterly useless on a fact-finding expedition into untamed terrain. If she talked about complaining to her father just once more, Tomas knew he'd snap and send her packing back to him. Probably in a crate. Nailed down. With a note to have it stored in the deepest archives of the *Pinakothek* as an example of Aboriginal artwork, not to be opened until he returned. Which, if he had any sense, wouldn't be for another few years.

Rain or nagging?

Poverty or *Papi's* money?

Tomas wasn't proud of this, but the old Graf Feldner's money went a long way, so Roderika had to be tolerated.

Her didn't love her that much, after all. And he was pretty certain the (lack of) feeling was reciprocated.

Certainly today they were.

She had moaned at two of their workers for not covering her hair, and shouted at their long-suffering *Diener* for not supplying her with sensible footwear (the poor man had actually tried that morning but she had been adamant that going out in flat soles was unbecoming of a lady). Now she had a broken heel, her feet were caked in dirt and her hair was no longer fashionably up, but hanging damply down her shoulders and covering one eye. In any other situation, Tomas might have found this funny, but he had learned not to laugh at his wife's misfortunes.

The trouble was he had made the mistake back at the Colby Hotel of telling their son that he was going to find treasure in the mountains. He was looking for a rock that many years of research, poring through ancient texts, the aboriginal writings (such as they were, being mostly modern transcriptions of generational folk tales) and studying the ancient texts both at the Neues Museum in Berlin and the British Museum in London had confirmed was somewhere in the Katoomba area. Echo Point, in the shadow of the legendary Three Sisters to be specific. There were ancient stories that there had been a Fourth Sister once, another colossal prong-like rock formation, but that it had been destroyed by the arrival of the object Tomas sought.

On hearing the word 'treasure', Roderika had immediately cancelled her plans for a day in the salon, left Josef in the care of his tutor and insisted on coming with him to find the treasure.

'My darling, I'm not talking jewellery, or precious stones. Not that kind of treasure. No, this is something plainer. Legend calls it *die Glanz*.'

'Treasure is treasure,' Roderika had replied. 'If it is important enough to have come halfway around the world to this wretched wet place, then it will be a triumph for us to share in.'

'Our new Chancellor would be very excited if we could bring this back,' conceded Tomas. 'I was contacted by the Party—'

'Did they fund this then? Save my poor *Papi* from doing so?'

Tomas shook his head. 'But hopefully they may pay us something if we take *die Glanz* back to them.'

'What is it, then? Why would the Party be so interested?'

'They are rumoured to be interested in the occult and—'

Roderika had just let out a long, slightly cruel, laugh. 'You believe that? You believe that the Chancellor really believes in that nonsense?'

'Your father does,' Tomas replied. 'That's why we are here. He could see this coming, all those months ago, when we set off on this trip. He was getting us, getting you and Josef out of Dachau, just in case.'

'In case what?'

Tomas sighed. If only Roderika had half the political savvy of her father. 'Your father, me, you – we're just *Parteigenosse*, but if Von Hindenburg goes, and your father believes that will happen very soon, there is no telling what the Party will do. This way, we can keep on the right side of the *Reichsleitung* by giving them something they can examine, keep, lock away, and do whatever it is they do with objects such as this. I don't know. But your father wanted us safely over here, that's why he put me on to this mystery.'

Roderika was going to laugh again, but she could see there was something in Tomas's urgent delivery, something in his eyes, that said he might be right. '*Papi* was concerned for the *Sturmabteilung* – he said that we needed to protect Strasser. I thought he meant politically but...'

'Strasser, Rohm, they could fall if Von Hindenburg goes. We are safe here; Josef is safe here. For now. We should find this treasure and decide afterwards if we let the Party have it.'

'If the Party want it, the Party will get it,' Roderika said. 'How could you do a deal with them if you knew how unstable home is?'

Tomas's rage flared up. 'I did it to save us all. It will be better to have them on side than to become a victim.'

'*Papi*...?'

Tomas took a deep breath. 'By now he should be safe in Denmark or Sweden. A lot of the old families are heading there, hoping to find a haven.'

Roderika closed her eyes, and then smiled. 'Darling, you are talking nonsense. You make it sound as if people like my father have something to fear from the Party. We should go find this ridiculous treasure of yours and carry it back victorious to the Chancellor and his *Reichsleitung*, and we shall be rewarded handsomely. Come on, I won't have you fill Josef's head with your paranoid ramblings.'

And Roderika had yelled for Tomas's *Diener* to prepare her aforementioned shoes, coat and hat, as she escorted Josef to his tutor.

Thus it was that the Schneidter party was pushing its way through the wind and rain to the base of Echo Point, directly below the Three Sisters in the Jamieson Valley.

Tomas had to acknowledge just how impressive the area was. It was like a massive horseshoe-shaped enclave, enclosed on three edges by incredibly high rock walls packed with trees, waterfalls and other amazing sights. To the 'front', the open part of the horseshoe, the valley spread out as a massive rainforest, as far as the eye could see. They had started at the top of Echo Point, come down the treacherous Giant Stairway, pausing at the top to take in the breathtaking vista ahead of them. Even Roderika had commented on how beautiful it was – and as it stretched miles and miles away into the distance, the trees created a fantastic canopy over the ground, and the distant mountains seemed to shimmer with a blue in the haze. She asked if that was what gave the region its distinctive name.

One of their party, an Aboriginal walker called Lue that Tomas had engaged earlier in the week, explained that it was eucalyptus oil rising from the trees because of the sun's heat that caused the haze.

Roderika thanked him. At which point the heavens had opened, and her mood evaporated with their shelter as they began the long dangerously steep descent down the Giant Stairway.

Tomas was just glad Josef wasn't with them, to give Roderika more angst and excuses to moan.

Halfway down, Tomas's *Diener* tapped him on the shoulder and pointed back at their Aboriginal guide.

'Lue?'

But Lue was shaking his head. 'I cannot go further,' he said. 'This is our land, our heritage and you seek to disturb it.'

Tomas shook his head. 'I'm looking for one item, one object. I promise nothing else will be taken or disturbed.'

'Just one pebble taken is wrong,' Lue insisted. He hugged his open-necked white shirt tighter around him, like a chill had suddenly run through him, although the wind was no greater here than anywhere else.

'What's the silly little man on about now?' Roderika called up, and Tomas gave her a look that implored her to shut up and not insult Lue.

When he turned back, Lue was gone. By rights, even if he'd just turned around to walk back up, he should still be visible, but it was like he'd just vanished. Swearing at the loss, Tomas carried on down, weighing up the pros and cons if Roderika were to 'slip'.

His *Diener* caught his eye and smiled momentarily. Ordinarily, Tomas could dismiss him for such a breach of protocol, but frankly, he understood the poor man's frustrations at Roderika only too well.

And now, finally, here they were, at the base of the mountain, staring at, well, rock. Lots and lots of rock.

'Well?' a wet, angry, dishevelled Roderika finally said. 'Treasure?'

Tomas swung around and snapped back 'I don't think there's going to be a big red X with "Treasure Here" carved into the wall!'

Roderika, not used to hearing her husband talk that

way to her stood and stared opened-mouthed at him.

No, not at him, *past* him.

Tomas turned to follow her eye line.

'Oh, don't mind us,' said a man. Tall, mid-fifties, greying hair, long dark coat with a red lining, leaning casually against a tree, arms folded.

Next to him, a slightly younger woman, dark hair, black jacket and trousers, stunning dark blue eyes that twinkled with mischief.

'Wotcha,' she said.

Despite the rain, they seemed dry as a bone. OK, so the trees might be giving them some shelter now, but to get down here they had to have been exposed to the elements.

'Who are you?' Tomas frowned.

'I'm a friend, and this is my friend, Bernice.'

'I'm an archaeologist. Somehow being his friend rates a higher mention in my CV than what I actually do.'

'Sorry,' the man said. 'Touchy today, aren't we?'

Bernice just smiled at Tomas. 'You're looking for the lodestone, yes?'

'The what?'

The strange man and Bernice exchanged a look. 'Not the response I was expecting,' the man said.

'No, I thought it'd be more "Oh yes the lodestone for the Ancients of the Universe, can you help me find it, seeing as you're a brilliant archaeologist, amazing scholar of ancient artefacts and all-round genius at things involving trowels, little fluffy brushes and dirt under the fingernails." But I guess not.'

Tomas just shook his head, looking back at Roderika and the rest of their party. All of them were similarly staring gape-mouthed.

'I don't think he was impressed by your credentials, Benny,' the man said.

'I missed off the thing too about being a pretty good reader of human body language. I don't think Herr Schneidter and Frau Schneidter are getting along today. She's not sure which of us to give the more poisonous looks to.'

Roderika stepped forward, her angst and ill-humour about rain, mud, everything, gone. In her place was an imperious but powerful woman, the woman Tomas had first met and been impressed by all those years ago.

'I don't know who you are, or what you are doing here,' she said slowly and pointedly, 'but this expedition is my husband's. We are here to find the treasure and when we do it belongs to him. To us. To our family. It is not, and never will be yours.'

The strange man widened his arms as if to say 'No problem'. 'I assure you, Frau Schneidter, we are not here to take the treasure away with us. We want your husband to find it and do exactly what you say. Nothing more. We're just, oh, I don't know, call us observers.'

Bernice nodded. 'Making sure it all goes to plan and everything works out as it should. Oh, and your treasure's roughly over there, embedded deep into the lower strata,' she added helpfully.

Tomas, now oblivious to the weather himself, waved

his people over and started digging where the soil met the rock, as Bernice had indicated.

'Why do you believe these *Verrückte*?' Roderika called over.

'Because, my dearest,' Tomas replied, 'I have nothing to lose by doing so.'

Roderika Schneidter looked back at the newcomer and his friend Bernice. Bernice was examining her nails, whistling. The man was tossing a clod of earth from one hand to the other, getting dirtier by the second.

'And why should I not have you shot right now where you stand?'

The man looked up. 'Well, that's not very friendly.'

'Not at all,' agreed Bernice.

'Firstly, shooting us is probably illegal in Australia. I mean, it's probably illegal in Germany too, but it is 1934, so anything's possible, I imagine. And secondly, why shoot us? I mean all we're doing is helping.'

'Making sure history stays on the right track,' Bernice smiled.

'Oh, why did you have to go and say that,' the man sighed. 'Look at her now.'

And indeed Roderika was giving them her darkest stare.

'Last time I got a stare like that,' the man said, 'was from a talking bear from darkest Peru called Paddington. He gave good stares. Yours is pretty impressive on the Paddington scale. Eight or nine out of ten.'

'History?' Roderika repeated.

'And we're focusing on *that*.' The man shook his head. 'Honestly, Benny, think before you speak.'

'Says the man who didn't think before he spoke, and now we're here,' Bernice retorted. 'Pot. Kettle. Black.'

'History will show that we will find this treasure and take it back home, present it to the party, to the Chancellor,' Roderika said. 'And he will reward us for finding *die Glanz*.'

Bernice smiled. 'Ah, finally, the name is right. The Glamour.'

The strange man looked at her quizzically. 'You what?'

'Stop it!' shrieked Roderika. 'Stop your talking now!' She pulled a gun from her handbag. A vintage pearl-handled Smith & Wesson 'Baby Hammerless'. 'You will let us take this treasure, and we will all walk away from this!'

Bernice and the stranger took a step back, hands up defensively. 'Not a problem,' Bernice said. 'Believe us, we want him to find it.'

This stand-off lasted a few minutes while Tomas and his men scrabbled with trowels, spades and brushes.

'I didn't need a big X,' Tomas finally muttered. 'I just needed them!' He was pointing excitedly at the man and Bernice.

'Well, far be it from me to take credit…' the man started, but Roderika was having none of it.

'I said shut up!'

'Shutting up,' confirmed Bernice.

And at that point Tomas stood up. In his hand was an oddly shaped piece of rock, lines of tiny crystalline ridges networking through it.

Bernice blew air from her cheeks. 'That's it,' she said quietly.

Roderika heard. 'And how do you know? How do you know that treasure would be there, now, today?'

'It's been here a long time,' Tomas started, but found himself covered by Roderika's pistol. 'My love?'

'Give it to me!' she said, hoarse after her shouting. 'Now. Give it to me now. My father must have *die Glanz*! It will buy back his power, his status with the Party!'

The man was looking at Bernice, who shrugged.

'I'm not sure you should do that,' Bernice said to Tomas. 'Web of Time and all that. Record books show you pretty definitely dig it up and hang on to it.' She looked at Roderika. 'Curiously, the history books don't even make mention of the missus at all. Just you. And Josef.'

Roderika swung round to cover Bernice and the strange man. 'Don't you dare talk about my son!'

'Our son,' Tomas corrected.

And Roderika swung back and fired her gun.

To the Doctor all the shouting, the rain on leaves, the mumblings of the men and clattering of shovels as they repaired the ground where they'd been digging was irrelevant. It was the sound of the bullet leaving the chamber, travelling down the barrel and breaking the sound barrier as it spat out of the Smith & Wesson's front, through the air and powered into Tomas's left shoulder that scared him. Bernice's horrified 'No!' was lost in the tsunami of events that followed.

First, the shocked Tomas's jaw opened in pain and surprise.

Second, the newly uncovered lodestone – aka the Glamour aka the treasure aka Graf Feldner's future success aka the whole wretched reason the Doctor and Bernice Summerfield had travelled back in time to ensure that everything happened as it was supposed to aka that stupid lump of rock – dropped from Tomas's rapidly numbing hands and fell to the floor.

As it touched the ground, a massive energy pulse shot out, with Tomas frozen at the eye of the time storm. Around him was a violent chronal eddy.

The Doctor was himself caught by the outskirts of the time eddy. But he could withstand it all. Just because he was a Time Lord.

And then, in ghastly slow motion, the Doctor watched, unable to move fast enough, pushing against an interstitial millisecond of time, as the pulse struck the people standing nearby.

Tomas's manservant, plus the three workmen simply winked out of existence, their time streams instantly thrown into reverse – horrifically, not only did they cease to exist but they never had existed, instantly erased from causality, taking with them any progeny they had and any memories deep within friends and acquaintances.

Thinking quickly, the Doctor roughly shoved Bernice backwards, into the trees and out of the path of the vibrating, shimmering cone of temporal energy spilling forwards.

And he went forwards, into it, ignoring the battering his body was taking.

By the time the pulse hit Roderika Schneidter it had lost its initial fury and, in her case, rather than devolve time, it shredded it around her.

For the briefest of nanoseconds she flittered between how she was now, a 10-year-old child, a baby, an embryo, and a twisted old woman, a skeleton and, finally, atoms scattered for ever.

As the Doctor pushed against the pulse that acted like treacle surrounding him, he too saw the death of Roderika Schneidter, each change in her timeline etched into his mind's eye. He tried not to look but, like a driver passing a car accident, he couldn't help but watch. A fascinating example of the devastating things time energy could do to living matter.

He was aware that the men closest to Tomas had simply gone, and focused on remembering that they had ever existed, making that his mission as he inched forward.

Finally with terrific effort, he reached down and grabbed the dropped / dropping Glamour / lodestone.

As his Time Lord fingers touched the rock, the time eddy simply ceased and, next to him, Tomas moved at normal speed, flung back by the bullet that was actually travelling backwards out of his body, pulled back to where it had begun, in a gun that had stopped being there when Roderika had vanished.

Tomas looked at the Doctor, who scooped the rock up and slammed it into Tomas's hands.

'Never. Drop it. Again,' he snarled, with more anger than he intended.

Tomas was just staring at where his wife had stood.

'Roderika?' he asked, even though he must have known the answer to his unspoken question.

'Gone, with your men.'

'What men?'

The Doctor shook his head. 'Bernice?' he called.

She was at his side in a second. Her face betrayed that she wasn't sure quite what had happened but she was focused enough to know that something had, mainly because one moment she had been standing next to the Doctor, then she was flat on her back in a bush, and the Doctor was twenty feet away, all in the blink of an eye.

She saw Tomas hugging the Glamour. 'Temporal problem?' she guessed.

The Doctor nodded. 'Do you remember how many people were here?' he asked.

Bernice frowned. 'Odd question. You, me, Tomas and Roderika Schneidter.' Bernice realised Roderika was gone. 'Oh. Poor woman.'

'Poor three other men,' the Doctor, muttered and explained what had happened to them and their personal histories.

'But what if they were important? Or their descendants? Butterfly effect and all that.'

'Time will repair the breach as best it can.'

'Let's hope none of them were due to cure cancer, bring peace to Africa or build a chocolate theme park.'

The Doctor looked at her. 'Build a what?'

'Joking,' she said with a smile. 'Inappropriately,' she added.

He still looked at her.

She continued. 'Bournville still exists in the twenty-seventh century you know, although it covers the whole of Birmingham. Which is no bad thing cos no one misses Birmingham.'

'My wife?' Tomas was looking around sadly.

'She's dead,' the Doctor snapped. 'Her own fault, frankly. And yes, I suppose I should say I'm very sorry, but I'm not. All I care about is that you have that lodestone. Treasure. Whatever you want to think of it as. Your job is to give it to your son, make sure he gives it to *his* son – and yes, he'll have loads of kids, they'll call him the Rabbit of Ryde. You have to impress on Josef and he on his kids, and so on, the importance that this stays here, in New South Wales. They must guard it with their lives.'

Tomas just nodded dumbly, not really taking anything in other than the forcefulness of the Doctor's words. 'My wife is dead?' was all he could think to say.

Bernice sighed. 'Yes. And… and to stop that happening to millions of others, you have to protect that rock, the Glamour, and keep it secret from everyone but your son,' she lied. It was the only way to make sure he did as he was told. As he needed to do.

The Doctor was already walking back to where he had left the TARDIS. With a final look at the aghast Tomas Schneidter, Bernice followed.

The Doctor said nothing as they walked through the rain and mud until they finally saw the TARDIS in a copse. Standing in front of it was a man, dark-skinned, in a white shirt and chinos. The same one he'd seen in Darling Harbour. But in 2015.

'Hullo,' the Doctor said quietly.

'You have taken the Papinjuwari from the mountain?'

The Doctor paused, thinking about the word. 'You're not from New South Wales, are you?'

'I have travelled a long way to keep the valley safe,' was all he said. 'I am Lue.'

'I'm the Doctor. And yes, it's gone for ever.'

'From the land?'

'No, but from here. It cannot leave the land, not for many decades. But one day Benny and I will be able to take it back where it belongs.'

Lue nodded. 'Thank you.'

He began to move away, then turned back one last time.

'We shall meet again, Doctor.'

Then he was gone, seemingly melting into the shadows cast by the tall trees.

'That was interesting,' the Doctor said.

'You know what was more interesting?'

'What's that?' the Doctor said ushering Bernice in through the open door of the TARDIS.

'He knew your name.'

As Bernice walked past him, the Doctor gave a final look at where Lue had walked, but there was no sign.

'He did. He did indeed.' He gave an involuntary shudder,

which Bernice would have said was someone walking over his grave.

Which wasn't something the Doctor really wanted to think about.

9
Notorious

It was 22 December 2015, and Mr Thomas Gordon Taylor was not having a great day. Truth was, he wasn't even having a good one. Nope. It could be argued that he was having the worst day of his life, but that would involve omitting the day his wife told him the Rabbitohs had only come third in their centenary year. Or the day they missed his daughter's wedding because of the rain closing the airport. Or –

'So, anyway,' interrupted the cause of his Worst Day Ever, 'the Duchess and I were wondering if we could get access to the exhibit.' The Scottish man smiled, very insincerely, Mr Taylor thought. 'What with her needing to get back to England for the funeral of her late, lamented husband, and then open Parliament, and then attending Wimbledon – she just has to see Valentino get things started off on Centre Court…'

The Duchess leant in, smiling far more sincerely. 'I do so love dear Rudolph.'

'Rudolph?'

'Valentino. Great tennis player,' she added.

The man shot her a look.

'His parents, huge movie fans. Who knew two famous people would have that name in history?'

Mr Taylor sighed. He was pretty certain that the Queen opened the English Parliament and it rarely clashed with the tennis, and he'd never heard of an Italian tennis player called Rudolph Valentino. All that aside, what he really wanted to do was go home to his wife, his cat and the DVR-stored episodes of *Wonderland*. Therefore he opened his drawer and passed over a couple of VIP lanyards to the Scottish man. 'Valid till 8 p.m.,' he muttered. 'Go to Level 6 and one of the guides will let you in.'

The Scottish man and the Duchess rose graciously from their seats (was the Duchess actually bowing? To him?) and stood aside as Mr Taylor made his way out of his own office, then followed behind him.

The Scottish Man passed the VIP lanyard to the Duchess. 'Oh, Mr Smythe,' she said haughtily, rhyming 'Smythe' with 'tithe', 'one cannot possibly wear this over this magnificent dress. You must carry the passes for both of us.'

Mr Smythe raised his eyes to heaven, draped a lanyard over himself and carried hers.

As Mr Taylor made his escape, the last thing he saw was Mr Smythe escorting the Duchess to an elevator.

And he was on his way home.

In the elevator, the two were bickering again. 'Duchess?

You had to say you were a Duchess. What made you say that?' the Doctor was grouching as he stabbed the Level 6 button.

Bernice shrugged. 'I wanted to be a Duchess.' She pointed at the elaborate dress, straight out of *Pygmalion*, that she was wearing, courtesy of a Shimmer.

'It's 2015,' he replied. 'Not *Downton Abbey*.'

Bernice clicked her fingers. 'Yes! *Downton Abbey*. That's a TV show, yes?'

The Doctor grunted that it was. Bernice clenched her fist and punched the air. 'Yes! Ha, sucks to you Professor "Downton Abbey was the seat of power in the United Kingdom during the nineteenth century before Buckingham Palace" Duffy.'

The Doctor gave her a quizzical look, then added: 'No, actually, I don't want to know.'

But Bernice ignored him. 'Professor Duffy, at the Tol Academy, so-called expert on Earth During the Last Days of the Monarchy. Told him I knew more about that era than he did, but oh no, to him *Downton Abbey* is a documentary. Idiot.'

'The state of history education in the twenty-seventh century scares me,' the Doctor said as the elevator came to a stop.

'I was an educator in the twenty-seventh century, thank you very much,' Bernice harrumphed.

'My point. Made in one.'

Bernice led the way out, reasserting her Duchess persona as she strode past bemused museum staff. 'My valet has the pass,' she said, waving a hand airily back towards the Doctor.

He noted that she at least pronounced 'valet' properly, with the hard 't' rather than the commonly assumed idea it had to sound like someone was drunkenly talking about valleys.

The Doctor was hurriedly showing the passes to anyone who wanted to see them and a few who probably didn't, all the time making sure they were heading in the right direction.

As they went through doors, down corridors and up tiny flights of three or four marble steps, he had to acknowledge that Bernice had efficiently studied the blueprints Keri had transmitted from the future.

'This should be a doddle,' he said. 'Quick in and out job.'

This particular escapade had started shortly after they had returned from the 1930s.

Ruth had booked them a room at a hotel in the cheaper part of town, in the heart of Korean, Chinese and other heavily westernised Asian cultures. Bernice had immediately fallen in love with the place because of this opportunity to study the integration of Eastern culture into Western.

The Doctor was less impressed. The navy-coloured bedclothes gave the room a dingy feel and the pictures on the wall were of various badly painted landmarks, a watercolour of a boat on a lake and what was probably once the top of a commemorative box of chocolates for the wedding of Charles and Diana that had been crudely put in a frame.

After the third minute of discussion about this, Jack had sighed and suggested to Ruth they go and sort out some food.

Peter had been more concerned with the whereabouts of Cyrrus Globb and the Spyro weaponista – a concern the Doctor had shared.

'We know that the lodestone, Glamour, key whatever you want to call it – and I do wish we could all just settle on one…' the Doctor started.

'Key,' said Peter.

'Lodestone,' said Ruth.

'Glamour,' said Jack with slightly more camp than he probably intended – although the jazz hands didn't help his case.

'Either way,' Bernice had joined in, 'we know what we're looking for. We also know that it's in a museum run by a descendent of Tomas Schneidter. Sydney has a lot of museums and galleries.'

'We actually don't know for sure it is still here,' Jack said.

'Yeah,' Ruth added, 'we just hope it is.'

'We also hope that Globb and the others haven't found it first.'

'They haven't,' the Doctor said.

'What makes you so sure?' asked Bernice.

'The Pyramid Eternia – it hasn't moved, and the world hasn't ended.'

'Both good points,' Jack said. He smiled at the Doctor. 'I like the way you think.'

The Doctor got his phone out and called Keri the Pakhar.

'Good thing you've got that,' Ruth said. 'Handy gadget, solves all our problems.'

'No, that'd be the sonic screwdriver,' Bernice said. 'The phone is only as good as the person on the other end.'

'Who is very good,' the Doctor said quietly. 'Keri! How are we?'

Bernice looked at the others and gave them a look that said, 'If that's what he wants to believe…'

'Yes, thank you,' the Doctor was saying. 'We popped back to the 1930s, as you do, and witnessed a significant amount of death and destruction, as you predicted, but didn't change the future, just as I said we wouldn't.'

Beat.

'No, no because that would have been wrong and unravelled who knows what else between then, the various wars on this planet, the year k2 bug and now.'

Beat.

'Yes Keri, but I'm a Time Lord and I *do* know about those things. So we are now aware, thanks to your marvellous help, that the Glamour is here in 2015 and we now know who has it. One of his descendants.'

Beat.

'No, no we don't know which one. That's what I need you to find out. Which one of them runs a gallery or museum in 2015 and where is it?'

Ruth clicked her fingers and tapped the bedspread a couple of times, jabbing furiously at the material.

The Doctor frowned.

Then Ruth ran to the picture on the wall from the Royal Wedding and pointed at Charles.

The Doctor nodded. 'Oh, of course, *blueprints*! Keri, when you find out where it is, I need the blueprints for the building.'

Beat.

'I don't know why. Ruth just asked for them.'

Beat.

'I don't know that either, really. She's a friend of Benny's.'

Beat.

'Yes, I'm always amazed to discover she has any too.'

Beat.

'Yes, she seems to be giving us both a non-verbal message which I suspect is neither polite nor especially mature. Oh and she's doing it again. Now, call me back when you have the information please.'

The Doctor hung up.

'We should go,' Peter said suddenly, a blaster rapidly appearing in each hand.

Jack, Ruth and Benny were up and alert instantly, which impressed the Doctor. For all the banter, all the laissez faire, they clearly knew how to work as a team when necessary.

'What's up?' he asked, swept up by their alertness.

'Globb has found us,' Peter said.

'How?'

'No idea.'

'How do you know?'

Peter tapped his canine-like nose. 'Kik the Assassin is very distinctive.' Peter cocked his head to one side. 'Not in the building yet, but they must have a tracker somewhere...'. Peter began patting his clothes down, and after a second he produced a tiny transmitter from his shoulder. 'Stupid! She must have put it on me outside the Opera House.'

'We should get away from here,' Ruth suggested but Benny shook her head. 'Better to play them at their own game.'

'How do you mean?'

Benny grinned. 'Globb's a con artist, allegedly one of the best. But so am I.'

'You're not one of the best, Mum. You're pretty far from being one of the best.'

'Oh I don't know,' the Doctor said. 'She fooled a lot of people into thinking she was a real professor.'

Everyone looked at Benny. Including Peter. 'I'm sorry?'

'When I first met Benny,' the Doctor said, perhaps enjoying this too much, 'she wasn't really a professor; she just told everyone she was to get to a planet called Heaven. And everyone believed her. She's very good at lying.'

'That was supposed to help was it?'

'Truth can't hurt us,' he smiled.

Bernice addressed the others. 'Obviously I am a professor now. I mean, I did it properly afterwards, once

I'd stopped hanging out with tall, grey and Scottish over there.'

'You know, I've never had proof she's a real professor,' Ruth said.

'Nor me,' Jack agreed. 'Everyone called her Professor, so I did too.'

'If my mum says she's a Professor, she's a professor,' said Peter.

'Thank you, darling,' Bernice said smiling.

'Anything to shut you lot up and get going,' he said back.

'So what's the plan?' Jack asked.

'Play Globb at his own game, convince him we're going to give him the Glamour.'

'Key.'

'Lodestone.'

'Whatever.'

'Why?'

'Because then he'll give it to us.'

Why will he do that exactly?' asked Ruth.

'Because I'll con him into thinking that's what he wants to do.'

'Why don't we just get it ourselves? Leave them out of it?'

'Because this way, we'll get him legitimately off our backs. And one other really important reason.'

'Getting them away from this time and place and back to the fifty-first century where they belong,' Ruth suggested.

Bernice shook her head, and smiled, her eyes glittering

like candles in the dark. 'That's *a* reason, Ruthie, and a good one – but not the *best* one.'

'And the "best one" is?' asked the Doctor, suspecting he already knew the answer, and indeed found himself mouthing the next words along with Bernice:

'Because it's fun!' She winked at the gang. 'The con is on!'

The meeting was arranged for an hour later. Peter had been the go-between, handling Kik the Assassin who in turn relayed information back to Cyrrus Globb and Professor Jaanson.

The two groups met in Darling Harbour, Peter having led them away from the Opera House where, all these hours later, they were still staring at the Pyramid Eternia in its new, hopefully temporary, home. This was because Jaanson wanted to see it in a new environment, and because he was also pretty dazzled still that he'd even found it.

Globb was far more intrigued by how they had travelled in time. He'd not travelled in time before, he explained to Peter as they walked. Peter explained it wasn't an everyday occurrence for him either.

Only Kik the Assassin said and did nothing except stare at Peter in a pretty annoying way that freaked the lad out somewhat.

'Wasting your time,' he muttered to her again.

When they met up with the Doctor and the rest of the team, the area around Darling Harbour was pretty empty – everyone, tourists and locals alike, having flooded down to Circular Quay and other Harbour Bridge areas to get a glimpse at the weird pyramid.

'What do you want?' was Globb's opening gambit, his usual charming self.

'You, sir, are a well-known conman,' Ruth said, pulling herself up to her five foot two height against his six-something-very-tall-indeed. He looked down on her like he might a bug he wanted to stomp on. But Ruth didn't flinch. 'Our team want to make you an offer – help us find the Glamour and we'll split the proceeds back in the fifty-first century between us, equally. Which,' she said with a look to Bernice that implied she thought this was a mad move for a group of successful con artists to make (and made sure Globb clocked it), 'means that that's a two-way split – fifty-fifty, half and half, tit for tat—'

Globb put a pudgy hand on Ruth's head to stop her talking. 'I get it,' he said. Then he looked at Bernice. 'I thought you were an archaeologist?'

Bernice threw her arms wide, but again it was Ruth who spoke. 'Benny is, like you, an expert at the long con. We've all been pretending to be a successful freelance archaeology team, going from planet to planet, finding rarities and then selling them on, usually the same piece to four or five gullible marks, making sure that we don't sell it to them within twenty-four hours of the previous one.'

'Such as?'

Ruth threw a look to Bernice but still spoke confidently, assuredly. Boy, she was good at this. She started counting on her fingers.

'Aloysius D. Campling, the Estatelands of Salvadori, Les Sourire du Starship Louvre, Jared Jones – we even sold stuff to the Braxiatel Collection…'

Globb nodded. 'I never heard of half of them. And I've never heard of you, and I know most of the teams working my quadrant.'

'The clue there,' interjected Jack, 'is "most". We're not a big gang but we're growing.'

'Nah, don't like this deal. Too risky.'

'Then how, dear sir,' said Jack, 'do you propose getting back to your time?'

'Why would I do that?'

And that was something Bernice and her team hadn't anticipated.

At which point Bernice stepped forward, and Kik the Assassin tensed, ready to protect her charge. Peter snarled, quivering his lips, showing some fierce canines. Kik the Assassin grinned at him, as if acknowledging his defence of Bernice, and stepped back. This little power game wasn't witnessed by anyone other than the Doctor.

'Nah, lissen mate, this is my job, this is my gaff, and I'm callin' the shots, yeah?'

Globb frowned. 'You what?'

Bernice shrugged and spoke in a broad East London accent again. This finally caused the Doctor to look at her in shock.

'I could ask you the same thing, guv. I didn't ask you to follow us here, this is my turf, innit. So, if you don't wanna be part of our proposal then, get orf my planet.'

The Doctor was still staring at her.

Bernice looked at him and hissed. 'Barbara Windsor? *EastEnders*? "Get aht my pub"? No? You're not getting it? Seriously?'

The Doctor finally spoke. 'Have you completely lost the plot?'

'You really think you can stop Cyrrus Globb?' asked Jaanson who, it seemed quite likely, had never even heard of Globb three hours beforehand.

'This is my team,' Bernice said. 'This is Shortie, she's my logistics expert. That's Dog-Boy, my personal security. Over there is Legs, he's a comedian and good with things that go "bang". And they call me Da Trowel, cos I'm good at diggin' up information.'

Globb looked at each one in turn, then jabbed a finger towards the Doctor.

'And remind me who is this? I don't remember seeing him on Aztec Moon,' he boomed angrily.

'That, my darlin', that is the leader of this little entourage, this group, this gang. He was waiting here for us because we set all this up. You see, Cyrrus Globb, that is the man wanted on every civilised world for cons and grifts of the highest order. This is the leader of us all, this is the brains of this outfit – surely you've heard of the legendary Doc Tardis?'

All the Doctor could do was take yet another of those deep breaths that Bernice provoked in him, and count to ten. Slowly.

*

Thus the Doctor found himself deep within the exhibit rooms of the Power Station, a six-storey Victorian building attached to Hyde Park, and overlooking the Bay. Just.

It was a name only the Australians could give to a museum of important artefacts, managed and run by the afore-met Mr Thomas Gordon Taylor. Taylor was the direct descendant of Tomas Schneidter and who, it transpired upon reading the guide to the Power Station, had zero knowledge of the Glamour / lodestone / key that his great grandfather had fought so hard to find – and sacrificed so much for. Instead it was listed as 'local unusual geological object found in the Blue Mountains National Park, not formed of basalt left by volcanic flow as per most indigenous rocks. The origins of this item remain shrouded in mystery. It may have significance to the Indigenous People, but if so, it has not been recognised as significant or culturally important by AIATSIS.'

'Wonder what our friend Lue would think of that,' said the Doctor.

Bernice just shrugged and checked her stopwatch. 'Everyone should have gone home by now, so we should make our way to the Glamour.'

The Doctor reached out for the stopwatch. It reminded him of the one Jack had used earlier. 'Do I get one of those, you know, now I've been co-opted onto your team of conmen?' he asked sourly.

Bernice shook her head. 'Have to be earned.'

'I don't actually want one,' he muttered. 'Mainly because I don't actually want to be here. I don't want to be a grifter.

I don't want to be responsible for committing a crime, and I don't want to be dressed up like some idiot at an Eighties throwback party.'

Bernice beeped his nose. 'Yes you do. You're loving this.'

'Am not.'

'Am.'

'Not.'

'You are. You know how I know you are?'

'Oh, do tell me,' he said.

'Because you're the Doctor, and the Doctor I know, no matter what his face, loves a bit of mystery, fun, adventure and universe-saving-from-extinction. It's your modus operandi. You might be the only leopard who can actually change his spots, but the analogy still holds – it's what and who you are.'

The Doctor looked at her. 'In your timeline, when did we last meet before all this kicked off?'

'Years ago. On Skaro. Ace stole an Omega device.'

'Skaro. Oh yes. I was very different back then,' the Doctor said quietly. 'I have been through hell, literally. A war with the Daleks that destroyed Gallifrey, leaving me pretty much the last of my kind. Billions of people, from all races and planets were affected, I watched stars burn, and galaxies implode. I faced terrible decisions and in the end when I took a chance, I broke every law of time and rewrote history. I saved Gallifrey as it was by then, probably changed the future for countless people and planets. But it still didn't get me home, didn't bring my people back to me. Friends and family, perhaps they live again, but I'll never know, Benny, because I can't find them. Beforehand, I knew that Gallifrey and the Time Lords were gone. Now I know they're not but I don't know what state I have left them in. In many ways, that feels worse.'

'It isn't, though, is it,' Bernice said, holding her oldest friend's hand gently. 'Because as always, you did the right thing in the end.'

'But I want answers,' he said. 'I want to know – I need to know. I feel… incomplete not knowing. Beforehand, I knew. I could move on, deal with things. Now it's just an endless jump from one planet to the next, hoping I might accidentally find a clue, stumbling in the dark. My friend Clara – you'd like her, she's clever and chirpy and infinitely rude to me, just like you – Clara said I was miserable and waspish once. And she was right. It's like I don't feel complete, for the first time ever. Once I had roots, then they were taken away. Now, I probably have those roots again, but they are out of reach.'

'And one day, you'll get them back.'

'How can you know that? Why say that if you don't know?'

'Because,' Bernice said quietly, 'I have faith. In the universe. It makes things right. You know why I think that?'

'No, go on, amaze me.'

'Because you told me that, when I was at my lowest. After a man I loved died and you were there to look after me – you went to extraordinary lengths to understand my grief and to empathise. I have never forgotten that, even though I know you must have because you've had so much in your life to deal with and so many people to remember. But I never want to forget how kind you were to me after he died.'

The Doctor took a deep breath and closed his eyes. 'Every time I visit France, I think of Guy de Carnac and what he sacrificed, Benny. No, I never forget the ones that truly matter.'

Bernice hugged him then, tightly.

'Hugging, again, everyone does the hugging thing. I don't do hugging, really.'

'Right here, right now, you do.'

And presumably recognising defeat, but perhaps also recognising a rekindled friendship borne out of tears and triumph many years ago, the Doctor returned the hug for a few moments.

Outside the Power Station, Ruth and Jack watched the windows from across the road, hiding in a doorway, hoping no one would notice them. Which was unlikely as they were in the heart of a city that rarely sleeps and, as they were discovering, was populated by people who never went home.

'It's 2 a.m.,' Ruth said. 'Why aren't they asleep?'

Jack was watching a young couple making out in another doorway. 'We used to be like that once.'

'Like what?'

'Young, happy, in love, unable to bear being parted, just for a few hours' sleep.'

'We're still like that,' Ruth said quietly. 'Except I can totally bear being apart for a few hours. But that's to do with the snoring and the legs.'

'Legs?'

'Yeah, those huge long things are pretty much the length of my body, and at night they kick. When you dream, you fidget. And kick.'

'I do not.'

'How do you know? You're asleep. I'm not, I'm awake. Being kicked by giant grasshopper legs.' At which point, deciding this conversation was no longer necessary, Ruth stepped out onto the pavement.

'What are you doing?' Jack hissed.

'My job,' she replied. 'Our job.'

'Which was what?'

'To keep an eye out and then do the thing.'

Jack pulled a device out of his pocket. 'Who knew Benny carried things like this with her?'

'Anyone who pays attention to what she said back in the White Rabbit on Legion, I imagine.'

'I pay attention!'

'Clearly not enough. Now come on, we need to be on the roof by two-fifteen local time.'

Jack watched as the happy couple down the street finally stopped kissing and moved quickly away, probably aided by him making a loud throat-clearing sound and ensuring that, when they looked at him, his red eyes glowed more brightly than normal in the dark.

He gave a final look around, grabbed his fiancée

around her waist and leapt the height of the old Victorian building.

Almost.

What he actually did was scale four storeys with ease, but the last two were a bit awkward. He'd later say it was Ruth's fault, that he wasn't carrying the additional – he was sensible enough not to use the word 'weight', even though Ruth weighed very little as she was so small, but foolishly he did tell one person the story later and instead said 'baggage', which went down like a lead balloon. But the gist was there.

And now so were he and Ruth, clinging on to a ledge four storeys above ground, silently. Ruth's wide eyes widened further as she looked down, and then realised Jack was holding on to the ledge with only one hand – the other of course safely holding her waist.

'And now what?'

Jack considered this.

Which was unusual for Jack – he didn't 'do' consideration; he was more an instant reactor to situations. 'Go deal with these people who haven't paid their bills,' his father would say, and off he'd go, ready to face whatever hoodlums, Mafiosi and dark underworld characters owed the firm cash. 'Go take this exceptionally dodgy-looking package that could be a bomb or the severed head of another crime lord's girlfriend to that war-torn planet in the irradiated sector that no one can survive more than thirty seconds in,' was another one of his father's suggestions. After a while, it occurred to Jack that perhaps his father and his brothers and sisters wanted him out of the firm. Permanently. Dead.

It was one of those things he had been going to talk to them about when, on a mission for his dad, Jack had become embroiled with Bernice and Ruth for the first time. Then he'd lost track of them for a while. Then he'd found them. Then he'd found time-splintered alternative reality versions that weren't actually alternatives but just perfect duplicates. (Or maybe the originals and the ones he was now hanging out with were duplicates, who knew?) Either way, Jack's involvement with Bernice and Ruth was fraught, frequently dangerous and usually involved Jack wanting to take Ruth away to some quiet leisure planet, get married and settle down, as far from Legion, guns, crime lords and his home world of Kadept as he could, and be happy. It was all Jack really ever wanted – to be happy. Ruth made him happy. So why was he now thousands of years in the past on a planet he didn't like, helping Bernice and a strange grouchy man with an accent he couldn't really understand, and hanging dangerously off a tall building, knowing that the slightest misstep could kill Ruth?

Oh yeah, because he couldn't say no.

Jack loved Bernice, absolutely. Great mates. But one day he really would have to say to her that it was fine if she wanted to go off and be all clever and adventurous, but to do it by herself. Or with Peter. But not him or Ruth.

'You'd better be thinking of a way out of this, Jack,' Ruth said, 'and not daydreaming again.'

'Again?'

'You do that, you drift off. In moments of stress, you just cease to be in the present. It's very annoying. It's also endearing at times and probably a great self-preservation thing, but at other times, like when you're about to drop your wife-to-be from a height she's not likely to survive, it can be a disadvantage.'

'I was thinking about that actually,' he said. 'About it being a disadvantage. Mind you, being here in the first place might also be considered a disadvantage – and I'm not talking about hanging from this building. I'm talking about being on Earth.'

'What?'

'Well, when we get home – and I'm sure we will because Benny and this Doctor bloke seem to be pretty good at all this and haven't died yet – can we just say, "Thanks, Benny, but no thanks"? Go somewhere, get married, have kids, live a nice life away from Legion and grow runner beans, breed cats, watch old episodes of *EastEnders*, that sort of thing.'

'What?'

'*EastEnders*. Haven't you seen Benny's collection? She's got every episode except the live ones.'

'No, I meant "What?" to the rest of it.'

'Oh. You want to stay on Legion?'

'Pretty much, yeah.' She looked at Jack, his dark red eyes, little pointy chin and sharp ears. 'Then again, what you want sounds kind of good too. But…'

'There's always a "but", isn't there. I don't like "but". A Ruth "but" leads to unhappy Jack,' he said.

151

'But, let's pick a world not too far away so that if Benny or Peter or any of our other friends need us in an emergency, we can get there pretty fast. Deal?'

Jack kissed her. 'Deal,' he said, and then suddenly leapt straight up in the air, grabbing a startled Ruth and did an amazing back flip that resulted in him landing easily on the flat roof, and lowering Ruth down beside him.

'You planned that all along, didn't you?'

'You thought I couldn't get us out of that situation, didn't you?'

Ruth kissed him again. 'One day, I'll stop thinking about what I think you can't do and think about all the things I think you can do. Like making me happy.'

And with a smile, Jack went into business mode.

Before them was a skylight, raised in a sort of triangular shape. He took the device Bernice had given him and with it he silently cut a small circle of glass. Then he cut a bigger one, and then a bigger one, all the time making the original hole larger but in increments so the glass wouldn't shatter. Eventually it was big enough to fit a reasonably small human through. Jack, being neither small nor human, wasn't going in. Beside him, Ruth had attached a cable to a belt around her waist and the other end around a brick chimney.

'Hope that holds out,' Jack muttered.

'It's been here two hundred years, through thick and thin,' smiled Ruth. 'I don't think it's going to crumble to dust tonight.'

With the glass safely cut away, Ruth took a pen-sized

laser cutter out of her pocket and jumped through the hole. The cable slowly extended, on a ratchet, so, rather than dropping through the air, Ruth lowered herself, lying flat, face down.

'I saw an old movie where they did this once,' Ruth said into a Bluetooth contraption pressed into her ear.

'The art of this manoeuvre is to be in and out, quickly and silently,' said a gruff Scots accent in both her and Jack's ears.

'Yes, "Doc",' Ruth said. She stuck the laser-cutter in her mouth, using her arms to balance her slow but steady descent.

Having waited quite a few hours till the Power Station was empty of all life (bar a couple of momentarily intrigued spiders and a cockroach and three security officers), the Duchess and Mr Smythe had emerged from their hidey-hole (a rather tight janitor's closet) and made their way to the Security Room.

This was clearly misnamed – the room wasn't secure, and the security guards weren't in attendance. The former was down to incompetence; the latter to a strong dose of laxatives Bernice had slipped into the milk in their kitchenette (both soy and normal, just to be sure) some hours earlier.

Their VIP lanyards, which had got them into the more private areas of the museum and thus to the closet, were now discarded, as were their Shimmers. Thus Bernice's outrageously OTT clothes were no more, and she was back in black. The Doctor was in his usual trousers and long coat.

His spare sonic screwdriver taking care of any cameras that might spy on them, they made their way into the security office, and Bernice created a fifteen-minute loop on their recording equipment that oversaw the Glamour.

They had opted not to take out all the cameras in the museum – that might draw attention. So they only took offline the immediate ones between the closet and the Security Room – the rest went into loops of empty corridors.

The Doctor froze – footsteps were approaching. Had one of the guards defeated his laxative ailment? He looked at Bernice. 'Three hours, you said!'

'It affects annoying White Rabbit customers for that long,' she hissed back.

'How many of them are overweight, underpaid security guards from Earth?'

'None of them.'

'Great trial subjects then,' he said. 'I'll go and deal with him.'

'How?'

'I don't know. This is your plan, not mine. I'm making this up as I go along.'

'So am I,' Bernice admitted.

'Oh that's just great,' the Doctor said, and left the room while Bernice finished her video sabotage.

'Hullo there,' the Doctor said, regretting ditching his VIP lanyard immediately. 'I appear to have got lost.'

The guard gave him a strange look. Then an even stranger one as something small was pressed against the skin on the back of his neck and he collapsed to the floor unconscious. As his body dropped, it revealed Peter Summerfield standing behind him, a little black box in his hand.

'What are you doing here?'

Peter grinned. 'Watching your backs. I followed you in hours ago. Had to laugh at your choice of hideout – a janitor's room? I just stood behind a big statue. No one noticed.'

'Your mum never said you were coming.'

'His mum didn't know,' Bernice said coming up behind the Doctor. 'What are you doing here?'

'I just asked him that,' the Doctor said. 'Do you know in all my years travelling through time and space, I don't think I've ever heard a question asked as often as "What are you doing here?" "Who are you?" and "It's bigger on the inside" come a close second, though.'

At this point, Ruth's message came through, the Doctor responded, and they made their way towards the room where the Glamour was kept.

On arriving at the imaginatively named Rock Room, the Doctor stopped Peter and Bernice entering. Taking out his sonic screwdriver, he calibrated it to sense the lasers that formed the protective net around the exhibits.

The security guards were a bit rubbish, but the actual items within the museum were expertly protected by state-of-the-art lasers and motion detectors. That was why Ruth was doing her *Mission: Impossible*-style entry from above.

'Ruth, you need to be very careful. Unlike in those movies, the sensors here go up as well as across. It's a proper lattice surrounding the security-glassed casket the Glamour is in.'

Ruth said nothing.

'Why isn't she replying?' Peter asked, furtively glancing behind them in case the other two guards, free of their toilet entombment, had found their unconscious chum.

'Her mouth is full of laser cutter,' Bernice said.

'She could nod or something,' Peter mumbled.

'If she does, those Bluetooth things might fall out and set off the floor alarms. I keep telling the Head of Security on Legion that we need something more secure, but does he listen? No, he says, "Yeeeees, Mum," and ignores me. But I'm right, aren't I, Mr Head of Security?'

'Yeeeees Mum,' said Peter and went back outside to keep watch.

The Doctor was carefully watching Ruth as she came down. He instructed her to take the laser cutter and carefully start layering away the glass, but make sure she didn't blow dust away or the alarms would go off.

Then everything shook.

Not just the room, but also the building. Not just the building, but also the street. In fact, Sydney rocked, quite literally, for a few seconds.

Everyone stared at the Doctor.

'You're assuming I have answers,' he said.

Bernice and Ruth nodded.

'At a guess, only a guess, the Pyramid Eternia has decided it doesn't want to be here any more, it's out of time and space and is about to blow up, taking Sydney, Australia and then Earth with it.'

'Starting a chain reaction that'll eventually wipe out the universe,' Bernice added.

'Not eventually,' said the Doctor. 'Pretty quickly. Shockwaves back and forth in time and the universe is rewritten in a split second.' He looked at Ruth. 'We really need to get that key thing back inside it and forget all this stuff with Cyrrus Globb and co.'

'Really?' said Cyrrus Globb. 'And why would you do that?'

The Doctor and Bernice turned to find Peter on his knees, Kik the Assassin aiming a gun at the back of his head, and Globb and Professor Jaanson, hiding behind the bigger man's frame, watching them.

'You can't keep us out of anything,' Jaanson stammered.

The Doctor turned to Globb. 'Look, I really don't understand what it is you want here. But I should have thought not being stuck on Earth would be foremost in your mind.'

Globb grinned. 'I'm not in prison here. Seems a great place to be.'

'What about her?' The Doctor pointed at Kik the Assassin. 'Your friend's hardly going to fit in.'

Kik the Assassin nodded at Globb. 'Not his friend; he's my bounty.'

'Oh,' the Doctor said. 'Well, yes, that makes sense.' He tapped his ear. 'Ruth, we can't risk another burp from the pyramid. Forget subtlety, OK?'

At which point, Ruth flipped over and kicked at the glass casket, shattering it, flipped back, scooped up the Glamour and shot back into the sky.

Globb, Kik the Assassin and Jaanson all followed her movements in surprise, as an awful lot of loud shrieking alarms went off.

The Doctor grabbed Bernice's hand and ploughed past Globb and Jaanson, running for the exit.

Peter tried the same, but Kik the Assassin, sat on him. 'Told you you'd be mine,' she hissed.

Globb and Jaanson legged it as fast as they could after the Doctor and Bernice.

'If we don't get out, a lot of local security people are going to find us here and blame us for all this,' Peter said.

'Good,' said Kik the Assassin. 'That way, I get to spend more time with you.'

'Oh good grief!' Peter shoved back, then forward with his legs, sending Kik the Assassin crashing into a wall. 'Get it into your head, I am only interested in one person.' And Peter stared at her, barely breathing. 'His name is… was Antonio, and he died. When I'm ready to move on, believe me, I will, but it won't be with you.'

Kik the Assassin nodded. She finally seemed to understand. 'I'm sorry for you loss,' she said.

'Thank you,' said Peter, brought up his hand, stroked her cheek and then activated his little black box again. Her yellow eyes widened in surprise, anger then shut – she was out for the count.

As the two security guards ran in, Peter pointed at her unconscious body. 'Call the police,' he said. 'She's armed and dangerous but will be sleeping for a good half-hour.'

'Don't move,' said one of the guards to Peter, rather pointlessly.

'Yeah, right,' Peter said, and faster than they thought could happen, Peter bounded forward, almost as if he were on all fours, like a giant dog, one of the guards would later report.

And he was gone, between their legs, down the steps and out of the building.

10
Other People's Lives

'I thought you said this was going to be "a doddle",' Benny said. 'Yes, I'm pretty sure "doddle" was the word you used.'

The Doctor looked at Professor Bernice Summerfield as they ran for their lives through the Sydney Central Business District. 'Seriously? I didn't even want to be here. But there's a gangster, his assassin and god knows what else after us, and you're quibbling over my choice of words?'

'No,' Bernice replied as they both swung round a corner, him using a lamppost as extra 'push'. 'No, I'm quibbling over the fact you thought this was actually going to be easy.'

'I don't think I've ever used the word "doddle" in my life,' he said, turning right into a small alleyway and stopping outside the back of a big building. 'Nor "quibble", for that matter.'

The nearest entrance was a huge black door, padlocked, with a few bins nearby. It was clearly the back entrance to a restaurant – Cuccurollo's, apparently. Tapas, perhaps?

Bernice stopped for breath, her hands on her knees as she sucked air in. 'You definitely said "doddle", but I'm so glad your priorities are about words and not dying in agony,' she said.

'You started this whole word thing,' the Doctor retorted. 'Don't blame me.'

There were yells and shouts from back in the streets.

'No one in Australia screams, they just yell and swear a lot.' Bernice grinned. 'I like this place.'

The Doctor nodded. 'Trouble is, it means your friend Augustus Gloop is close by.'

'Cyrrus Globb,' Bernice corrected. 'And he's not my friend.'

'Do you know,' the Doctor paused as he went to kick a door in. 'If I had a penny for each time over the years you've said people trying to kill us weren't friends of yours and it turns out they were, once, a long time ago, before you crossed them – I'd be a very rich Doctor.'

'You'll be a very dead Doctor if you don't get a move on!' She pointed at the door. 'Sometime this week would be good.'

The Doctor glared at her, sighed and kicked at the door.

It stayed resolutely closed but did so making a loud noise at the same time.

Bernice gave him an equally withering look. She eased him aside, smiled sarcastically and kicked at it herself.

It swung open, whatever lock it had sent spinning into the darkness beyond.

'Oh. Well, I weakened it,' he said.

'Course you did,' she smiled. 'After you.'

And they ran into whatever dark, dank building they'd just illegally gained entry to.

Had they waited a moment longer, they'd have seen Globb come around the corner, followed a second later by a puffing and panting Horace Jaanson.

'Well?'

Globb was standing still, a hand up. 'There!' He pointed at the door Doc and Da Trowel / that Summerfield woman had used.

Jaanson looked at him in amazement. 'I can see why they call you the best of the best,' he said, not hiding his disdain. 'I mean, a short, dead-end alleyway and a door kicked in. Gosh, I wonder where else they might have gone.'

Cyrrus Globb turned menacingly. 'Don't cross me, Professor.'

'Or what?' Jaanson grunted. 'You'll have your blue lady assassinate me?'

'Enough!' Globb slammed the little human into the wall, lifting him high off the ground, causing the Professor to squirm and dangle his legs uselessly.

'My dear sir,' he choked. 'I apologise if you mistook my gallows humour for rudeness. Absolutely unintentional. I have nothing but the highest regard for you and your criminal skills.'

At least, that's probably what he said – the last few words just came out as strangled gasps and wheezes.

Globb dropped Jaanson back to the ground. Still short of breath Jaanson waited for a moment until he was strong enough to get back to his feet. He held out a hand, hoping Globb would pull him up but Globb walked away, and went over to the kicked-in doorway.

'Not in there now,' he rasped, licking his fat lips in annoyance. 'We should disappear before the local authorities come searching for us.'

'Why would they do that?' Jaanson asked. 'And why do we care anyway? You can just kill them.'

'I don't kill locals.'

'Why not? You're happy enough to see them blown to bits when the pyramid destroys the planet.'

'That's different.' Globb smiled. 'I don't have to dirty my hands or reputation from a distance.' He smiled again, this time at Jaanson. 'Mind you, when a job is over I don't mind asking people like Kik the Assassin to tie up any… loose ends.'

Globb straightened his suit. 'Killing me would not be a good use of resources. We could have a future together, you, me, Kik the Assassin. We could pull off all sorts of crimes across the cosmos.'

Cyrrus Globb smiled the sort of smile that men like Horace Jaanson never felt comfortable around. Mainly because it implied threat, enjoyment of violence and a suggestion that they knew more than you did. Jaanson especially didn't like it because it was the sort of smile he had been given throughout his lifetime – at school, at university and even at work.

In the distance, a siren was blaring.

'The police are coming this way,' Globb said. 'We should go.'

'Where?'

'To the hideout.'

'We have a hideout?'

'We go to theirs.'

'They have a hideout?'

Globb reached a hand into his business suit's inner pocket and brought out a small black device. He scanned the skyline with the device and two buildings on the fascia glowed red. He tapped twice at one.

'Arcadia at Central?' said a sweet human female voice. 'How can I help?'

'Oh, hullo there,' Globb said in an equally sweet voice. 'Awfully sorry to bother you, but my business partner and I have arrived in the city and been badly let down by –' he quickly tapped the other red-lined building – 'the Campbell Tower, who seem to have lost our reservation. I really don't have the time or, frankly, the patience to deal with their incompetence. Do you have a room for tonight? Price is no object. I believe my... sister is staying there already, she recommended your establishment very highly.'

'Of course we can help you,' said the Arcadia's receptionist. 'I can have the rooms ready for you in ten minutes.'

'We're on our way.'

'What name is it?'

'Summerfield,' Globb said quickly.

'That'll be perfect, Mr Summerfield. Your sister's party have already booked in. Would you like a room next to theirs?'

'That would be very good indeed, thank you.'

'See you shortly,' said the receptionist.

'And how are we going to pay for a hotel in this time zone?' Jaanson asked.

Globb just strode along the darkened pavement. He casually walked into a well-dressed man, staggering home after a night out drinking. He apologised as Globb feigned a stumble. 'Not a problem,' Globb said, and the drunk man went on his way. A moment later, Globb repeated the same trick with a couple of giggling young women.

By the time he had done it to three more people en route to the Arcadia at Central, he had collected enough wallets and purses with enough cash to pay for a week's stay.

Peter was cleaning the apparatus Ruth had used to descend into the Power Station and grab the Glamour. It was like he was restoring an antique – the level of care and attention he was giving it made Ruth smile.

Ruth had known Peter for a year now, seen him grow from an angry teenager, bitter about his mother 'abandoning' him for a year or so, leaving him to fend for himself in a post-war slave pit until he was rescued. She understood some of that anger – it wasn't just aimed at Bernice, who couldn't help not being around for him, that was circumstance. The war they had both been through had separated them in time as well as distance. But there was something else behind Peter's pent-up aggression, his reason for taking on the job of Head of Security on Legion, and making it a success at 18 years old. The anger that propelled him forward back then had been a result of someone messing with his head, convincing him that his lover was still with him, every day sharing his home and bed. In fact, he'd died in the slave-pits of Bastion, a fact that had been exploited by a vampiric alien who had manipulated him for the next year. By the time Ruth and Bernice reached Legion, Peter was a bubbling cauldron of hate, angst and – although Ruth had never said this aloud to Bernice – insanity.

Time had healed them, brought Peter and his mum back together. Ruth, Jack and a few other friends had helped with that too. But at heart, Peter was a scrapper; he wasn't content unless there was a fight or battle to be won. Despite his youth, he was wise and experienced. He understood conflict, he read people's body language expertly (a trait he clearly inherited from his mum) and there were very few weapons he wasn't familiar with.

That was the bit that always alarmed Ruth. She wasn't good with guns; she didn't want to be, either. Her background, as far as she could remember it at all, was as a slightly submissive servant. Yes, there was far more to her than that, other aspects of her past that had been overwritten and distorted by the same vampire-creature that had affected Peter, but Ruth had chosen to focus on the life she recalled, as a worshipper of Poseidon, when she was happy in blissful ignorance. Her true history, where she came from, who she was and the things she did were something she didn't talk about.

Jack had tried, once, to get her to face that part of her past, but she had made it clear (as did the frosty side of their relationship for about a fortnight) that she was not inclined to think about it. However much of a lie the Poseidon thing was, it was a past she was happier to embrace.

That's how bad her real life had been.

So Ruth understood Peter, she liked him and treated him like a little brother – although there wasn't much between them age wise. A handful of years. Then again, Peter was part Killoran, so maybe in 'dog' years, he was older than 19. 'Dog' years, however, wasn't a phrase one used around Peter.

Everyone, it seemed, had parts of their past they'd rather ignore/delude themselves about.

Talking of which, Ruth looked up as Jack entered their hotel room, pizza boxes in his arms.

'Isn't it good to know that no matter how far back in time you go, pizza is still pizza.' He put them down, sitting cross-legged (in his case that took up some space) opposite his fiancée.

'Go back past the eighteenth century and it's very different,' Peter said. 'What we call "pizza" back home started around then.'

Ruth smiled. 'Pizza expert?'

'Archaeologist mum, with a passion for Earth. It's amazing what you pick up in idle conversation. My dad liked pizza. Hawaiian.'

Jack pointed at a box. 'There's one of those there, though I really don't get pineapple on pizza. Each to his own.' He stuffed something meat-based into his mouth and Ruth was sure his eyes momentarily glowed redder. He smiled. 'Jalapenos.'

Ruth didn't know what that meant so Jack went to pick one off a slice. 'Red or green, my lovely? What's your desire?'

'Don't,' warned Peter. 'You'll regret it.'

Ruth decided Jack wasn't out to poison her – it'd be a short engagement if he did – and she liked trying new things. She took one of each and popped them in her mouth.

And spat them out again, shrieking, while Jack literally rolled onto his back, kicking his legs, laughing raucously.

Even Peter managed a smile, Ruth could see, through her tears of burning-mouth-syndrome. He reached down and passed her a can of cola and she took great gulping mouthfuls of it.

'Mean, Jack,' Peter said. 'Dead mean.'

'But so funny,' Jack countered, still unable to get off the ground, he was so amused.

Finally Ruth was able to move and she leapt onto Jack, pummelling his chest with her small hands furiously, not sure if she wanted to break his ribs or move to his face.

Jack eventually stopped laughing and grabbed her

wrists. She struggled for a moment as he drew her closer. 'That was funny,' he said, grinning from ear to ear.

'Not to me, it wasn't,' Ruth said.

Jack pushed his head forward and kissed her on the lips. 'Oh, it so was, babe, it really was.'

'Get a room,' was Peter's response.

'Already got one.'

'Yeah, I feel welcome,' laughed Peter. 'Listen guys, look after that Glamour thing, yeah? I am a bit worried about that Spyro weaponista.'

'Finally got you to notice her?' asked Jack, managing to hold Ruth away with a long arm, as her fists flailed pointlessly in the air around his hand.

'Ha ha, Jack. No, she's a lethal trained killer, probably locked up in some local prison with a bunch of idiots she could kill before they even breathe at her.'

'She's not your problem, Petey,' Jack said.

'She is,' Peter said, as Ruth gave up and slumped on the floor, waving air into her mouth. 'I got her captured, I ought to get her back to the pyramid ready for Mum and the Doctor to do their magic with that rock thing.'

Ruth took the Glamour from her rucksack. 'I wonder what this actually is?'

'Didn't get a chance to see it in the future.' Jack nodded. 'Close up, it just looks like a rock.'

'It is a rock,' Ruth said.

'Maybe it's a bomb,' Peter said.

The other two stared at him.

'Well, if I wanted to create a bomb to blow up the

universe, I'd disguise it as a rock. Seeya.' And with a smile at their newly alarmed expressions, Peter slipped away.

Ruth and Jack were still staring at it, pizza getting cold when, ten minutes later, Bernice and the Doctor entered the room.

The Doctor stuffed some Hawaiian into his mouth. 'Cold pizza. My favourite. Not.'

Bernice was more concerned as to why Jack and Ruth, who normally couldn't be trusted with pizza, were sat dead still, staring at a rock with untouched pizza in boxes around them. 'Guys?'

'What if it's a bomb?' asked Jack.

'It's not a bomb,' said Bernice. 'Is it a bomb?'

The Doctor got his sonic screwdriver out, ready to scan it, but Jack knocked it away. 'It's a bomb.'

The Doctor threw him a tired look. 'It's a lodestone, a key. It's not a bomb.'

'It might be a bomb,' Ruth suggested unhelpfully. 'I mean, we don't really know, do we? It could be a bomb.'

'It doesn't look like a bomb,' Bernice said.

'Look,' the Doctor sighed. 'Can we all stop using the word "bomb". This is not a bomb. I mean, how does a lump of rock become a bomb?'

Jack and Ruth stood back, as Bernice stood up. She gave the Doctor a 'What on earth...' look, her hands spread out in exasperation. 'Are you serious?'

The Doctor nodded. 'Yes, yes I am. Look Benny, I appreciate your concern, but I absolutely know that's not a bomb.'

'How?'

'Because I'm the Doctor, and I know a bomb when I see one. That is a key. It's probably a pretty intricate and complicated and very definitely useful lodestone that can act as a trigger mechanism for the Pyramid Eternia, or at least the technology that the Pyramid Eternia represents, but it's not a bomb.'

'We're supposed to accept that,' Jack asked. 'Just because he's your precious Doctor?'

Bernice nodded. 'Yup, for no other reason. He says it's not a bomb, then it's not a bomb. He's always right.'

'Nearly always,' said the Doctor, maybe not at the most opportune moment.

'Nearly always?' Ruth queried. 'I mean how often is "nearly always"?'

'Pretty often,' Bernice said.

'Mostly,' the Doctor added.

Jack stroked his pointy chin. 'Define mostly.'

'A lot.'

'Quite a lot.'

'Nearly always.'

'We've done "nearly always", guys. Can we define our definitions better, please?' Jack stopped stroking his chin and put an arm around Ruth's shoulders. 'Do either of you actually have a clue what you're doing?'

Bernice nodded. 'He does,' she said, indicating the Doctor. 'And I do too. So you have a whole 200 per cent of clue-knowing marvellousness.'

The Doctor was suddenly behind Jack and Ruth and

went to put his arms round them. He realised that it was pretty much impossible to reach Jack's shoulders without tiptoeing or to reach Ruth's without bending down, so he gave that up and just pointed at the rock from behind them. 'That is a lodestone, a key, known locally as the Glamour. And it contains a great deal of power. If it was mishandled in any way, it could rip apart the entire universe, erase it in a second or rewrite it so that we're all related to frogs.' He looked at Jack's legs. 'You're more grasshopper than frog, aren't you? Great, brilliant, love grasshoppers. OK, so all of us, including Cyrrus Globb and Horace Jaanson, want this to gain entry to the pyramid that's currently changing the tidal flow around Sydney's waterways and really needs to be got rid of. But we don't want them to have it, am I right?'

'Well…' Jack started, but Ruth poked him.

'Yes, Doctor. We don't.'

'Thank you.' The Doctor shot Jack a look of venom. 'As I was saying, Bernice has a plan to keep this out of their grubby mitts.' He looked across to Bernice expectantly.

There was a silence.

Quite a long one.

In the grand scheme of pauses that no one wants to go on for quite some time, this was a doozy.

Eventually, Bernice shrugged. 'Why d'you think I have a plan?'

'Because, Professor Summerfield, you told me you had one.'

'No, I told you I had a plan to stop Cyrrus Globb getting

his hands on it in the first place and out of the museum. That plan worked: we now have the Glamour. But I haven't got a clue how to stop them coming to get it back.' She smiled at him.

The Doctor just stared at her with his big old eyes, mouth slightly agape. 'You roped me into this.'

'Because I knew you'd understand how the Glamour would work. And how to stop the universe going up in a big bang. Which you've done.'

'No, I've delayed it, apparently. That's all.'

Ruth and Jack looked at one another. 'I think maybe we should leave them to it – go find Peter.'

Ruth nodded. 'Absolutely. Peter. Needs finding. He usually does.'

'Bound to be in trouble of some sort.'

'Trouble. Always with the trouble that boy.'

And the two of them snuck out of the hotel room.

11

Last Day on Earth

Barangaroo Police Station was, Peter thought, a pretty dull place. Obviously – it was a police station, boring by definition. But this one really took the biscuit for sheer mind-numbing unimaginativeness. It was a concrete and glass affair that looked more like a library than a headquarters for law enforcement. It even had a small café area for people to wait in.

As Peter took in the reception area, he mentally ticked off the security-shy entrances and exits. A good concerted attack and this place could be under enemy control in less than eighteen seconds. The window to the left wasn't secure. The door to the cells was unguarded. The main entrance had no worthwhile locks or meshes to speak of.

And, above all, morons populated it. Well, maybe not all morons but Senior Sergeant Rhodes wasn't the sharpest tool in the box. His greying hair and engorged stomach suggested someone who had probably joined the force as a probationary constable as a teenager and had stayed there ever since. Peter sniffed slightly – the policeman smelled of stale sweat, alcohol and cigarettes, as well as thirty years sat on his behind, rather than getting out and catching criminals.

He was looking at Peter with a disdain Peter had got used to. After all, to the humans, he was a teenage thug in a tight hoodie, making sure his face was pretty much hidden by the oversized hood.

What the Senior Sergeant couldn't see, despite his thirty-odd years on the force and his pretty insignia with its stripes and crest, was that Peter was concealing more weaponry than Rhodes had probably ever seen in his life.

'So, you've come for your friend, have you?'

'She's not really my friend, but yeah, I need to get her out of here.'

The Senior Sergeant tapped a computer and brought up a CCTV-style image of the cells (more a comfortable room with a couch and coffee table). Clear as day was Kik the Assassin, sitting there, still as a statue, and Peter guessed she was probably trying to work out the stress on the door locks, or whether if she hit the wall with the side of her hand in the right place, she could cause a chain reaction that would bring the entire building down. For a pretty slight person, Kik the Assassin was pretty powerful, he thought.

He smiled. 'Look, Sergeant, you might as well let me take her away. Keep her here much longer and she'll probably tear this place down around your ears.'

The Senior Sergeant sighed and led Peter towards the

cell area. He pointed to a door with a small gap cut into it and now Peter could see Kik the Assassin properly. And she could see him.

She didn't move an inch.

'I've come to take you away from all this,' he said through the gap.

Nothing.

'There's paperwork to fill in,' the Senior Sergeant was saying. 'She needs to come back next week to sort out a hearing. And there's bail to be paid.'

Peter dug into a pocket and tossed a roll of plastic-coated bills at the police officer. 'That cover it?' And Peter realised that was a mistake.

'I hope that's not a bribe of some sort, mate,' Rhodes said, frowning at the money.

'Too much?'

The Senior Sergeant passed it back to Peter. 'Doesn't work that way in New South Wales.'

'You have a massive great pyramid in the water by the bridge, and you're worried about rules and regulations?'

'Yes. Yes, I am. Just because the world has gone to hell doesn't mean that law and order breaks down. If nothing else, it makes us stronger.'

Peter looked at the human with a fragment more respect. 'That's good,' he said. 'I can get that. Security is always important.'

'There are thousands of lives depending on the police, mate. Remember that.'

Peter nodded. 'I face the same quandary at home,' he

said. 'I'm the Head of Security there. That's a lot of people to control.'

'Oh, and where's that?'

'Legion. You won't know it.'

'Nightclub, is it? Use you as a bouncer or something? Coat check?'

Oh, and that was the momentary respect gone.

'Legion is a vile place,' Peter said quietly. 'Populated by thieves, murderers, fighters and smugglers. Just one of them could bring this city to a halt in an hour. You wouldn't stand a chance facing what I keep control over every day.' He pointed towards Kik the Assassin. 'People like her.'

Kik the Assassin looked up finally and smiled. 'I'm glad you recognise the threat I pose to you, and to this pathetic planet,' she said.

'You don't pose anything to me,' Peter said emotionlessly. 'And unlike my mum, I don't care about this planet, so you're no threat to me at all.'

Kik the Assassin stood up. The policeman took an involuntary step back, as if he saw something that told him she wasn't the docile, slightly weird emo-girl in weird blue make-up that he'd thought she was.

'Now hang on, you two, I thought you were friends...'

'Us?'

'Friends?'

'This pathetic mongrel has no friends,' Kik the Assassin said. 'Least of all me. I have broken out of stormcages that make this place look like a paper house. I need no aid from the likes of him.'

The policeman placed a hand out, and rested the other on his sidearm. 'Now, I'm not having any trouble from you two, right?'

'Wrong,' said Peter, a little sadly.

'Wrong,' said Kik the Assassin, a little too gleefully for Peter's liking.

Kik the Assassin jumped towards the door from a completely still, sitting position. The speed impressed Peter. The utter disintegration of the door impressed him less. With a sigh, he felt like chastising the senior sergeant on the ridiculousness of his supposed security. Then he remembered this was Earth – the average human would have been unlikely to be able to damage the door. But, like him, Kik the Assassin had been trained to spot weak spots, unseen fractures, the tiniest flaws in something, and use them to her advantage.

The shattering door had two advantages. Firstly, it provided her with a means of escape. Secondly, as it flew outwards, it took Senior Sergeant Rhodes out of action with it.

As he hit the floor unconscious, Peter heard the yelps of other officers back in the main precinct area. With a sigh of annoyance, he flicked his wrists down past his waist then back up, and now he had a blaster in each hand. The one in the left was a standard Deindum maser, capable of drilling holes in its target at anything from pencil-lead thickness to the size of a dinner plate. In his right hand was a gun of his own design that he'd spent a few weeks perfecting back on Legion.

The maser was kicked out of his hand and away into the corner as Kik the Assassin came past him, in a blur of somersaults and backflips. He had to admire the athleticism of it all.

He immediately put his left hand to the rear of his belt and brought out a Fifth Axis standard pulse gun, and fired to Kik the Assassin's right, spoiling her latest back flip, so she crashed to the floor.

'Two hands, three guns. Seems greedy,' she spat.

'Or just well prepared,' Peter grinned at her. 'You're hardly my first Spyro. Don't worry – it's only set on stun.'

And he ducked behind a filing cabinet and started crawling to a better position.

Kik the Assassin lay still, her reptilian head twitching from side to side, the scales around her nose expanding as she sniffed the air. Her yellow nictitating eyes widened and blinked as she hunted her prey. 'Mongrel,' she called, and lashed out with a foot, trying to upend the filing cabinet.

He saw it coming a mile off and did his own perfectly performed back flip, parkouring off the wall and back to a taut, ready-for-anything pose, but out of her physical reach, all in the time it took the cabinet to hit the ground.

Kik the Assassin reached down and scooped up his dropped Deindum maser and went to fire it.

Behind her, three police officers ran into the area, drawing their side arms.

Kik the Assassin was on one of them in a second, slamming his body against the wall, and she looked up at his wheezing face as it went purple, her head again jerking spasmodically side to side. 'On my world, we eat your kind as you snack on candy,' she said. She opened her jaws, wider and wider, until it looked entirely possibly that very soon she might indeed be able to swallow the policeman in one go.

Before Kik the Assassin could react, Peter almost lazily raised his homemade gun and fired.

Phut. Phut. Phut.

All three officers dropped unconscious where they stood.

To Peter's right, Senior Sergeant Rhodes stirred, saw his friends shot and immediately went to pull out his own gun.

Peter gunned him down casually and he flopped back to the floor.

Kik the Assassin swung away from Peter and instead shot at the wall to the outer precinct area, where more yells and screams were starting up. A segment of plaster and besser-blocked wall disintegrated, making the now visible police officers flinch and hide. She fired more rounds, shattering phones, laptops and TV screens, leaving sheets of paper floating sadly down to the floor, as the humans scattered, trying to find safety where this mad woman couldn't find them.

One of them didn't flinch and instead slowly and deliberately drew her pistol, holding it in both hands and aimed at Kik the Assassin and Peter, just moving the muzzle as she stared at each of them. 'This stops right now,' she barked.

Peter shot her expertly in the chest and she was flung back onto a desk and then the floor.

As the others recovered, Peter stunned them all one by one.

He realised a civilian was standing by the glass doorway in utter shock, his bags of shopping dropping to his feet.

With a sigh, Peter took him out as well.

Kik the Assassin was on all fours, spread-eagled like a cat or a spider, ready to bounce, every muscle locked in place, perfectly poised for action. As the noise and dust settled, she looked back at Peter and smiled. 'Hey, sexy.'

Peter raised his eyes to heaven. 'You what?'

'That was cool. Never knew you had it in you, mongrel.'

'Leave the "mongrel" thing out, yeah. Beyond the fact it's racist and offensive, I simply don't like it.' Peter shrugged. 'Don't like you much, either.'

'You are magnificent,' Kik the Assassin said, bounding over to him, making no attempt to disarm him, but instead throwing her arms around his waist and kissing him. On the lips. Quite passionately.

Peter extracted himself, bringing his gun up to her head height.

'Well, that's not quite the response I was expecting,' she said with a grin. 'I do like my men manly and powerful.'

'No, you like your men any way they are, provided you can get something out of them.'

Kik the Assassin shrugged. 'Oh don't be such a spoilsport. Besides, other than a kiss, what am I trying to get out of you?'

'Access to the pyramid, I imagine,' Peter replied. 'Especially as you just took what you probably think is some sort of keycoder from my back pocket.'

Kik the Assassin looked coy. 'This little thing?' she said holding up what she had half-inched from him.

'That little thing,' Peter confirmed. 'It's not a keycoder, by the way.'

'And what is it then, some part of your fake-grifting paraphernalia?'

Peter raised an eyebrow. 'You what?'

'Oh, Globb and I know what you lot are up to. Trying to pretend you are criminals, conmen, and we're your marks. But you're not; we saw straight through that. You can't grift a grifter like Cyrrus Globb.'

Peter thought about this. 'Is that so?' he said finally.

Kik the Assassin nodded her mohawked head, smiling widely. 'We had you lot marked out the moment your mother walked into the Pyramid Eternia on Aztec Moon. She's no grifter, she was looking for the Glamour, like that stupid Jaanson was. She should have had the word "ARCHAEOLOGIST" in big red neon letters floating above her head. Globb reckoned what she and your friend "Doc" know about short and long cons can be written on the back of my hand.' She held her hand up. 'And I have very small hands.'

Peter smiled. 'You got me, you got all of us.'

'I bet she's not even your mum. She looks human to me.'

'She is.'

'You're not.'

'I sort of am. My dad was Killoran. I was born on Deirbhile.'

'A Stormcage planet, yes?'

Peter nodded. 'Born there, brought up on KS-159, transported to the slave pits of Bastion, now living on Legion. I know all the best places it seems.'

Kik the Assassin pouted in mock sympathy. 'Poor mongrel boy. All that dark angsty childhood. How did you get caught up with all this?'

'She's my mum.'

'For real?'

Peter nodded.

Kik the Assassin absorbed this information. 'Well, I think you're pretty sexy and hot. For a moron, of course.' Suddenly, the Deindum maser was pointed at his face, and all trace of charm was gone from Kik the Assassin's face. She held up what she had taken from Peter. 'And I reckon, despite what you say, that this is a keycoder, probably to whatever ship you came here in. And as I have absolutely no intention of going back to the Stormcage, this is going to give Globb and me access to freedom.'

'You and Globb? Why?'

Kik the Assassin just shrugged. 'None of your business, mongrel.'

Peter nodded at the device. 'You're right of course. It is a keycoder. It's also a tracking device – it doesn't just let you into the Doctor's time ship, it tells you where he parked it.'

Kik the Assassin frowned momentarily. 'Time ship?'

'Yeah, steal it and programme it to get you back home. So long as you're careful, don't tread on any butterflies whilst you're here, you should be fine. Besides –' Peter waved his arms around the wrecked police station – 'it's not like you're human, so none of your ancestors are likely to be here.'

'But Cyrrus Globb has some heritage here. This could invalidate our contract.'

Peter laughed. 'Sorry. That's the risk you take coming to twenty-first-century Earth. Dirty, smelly, full of germs, inedible food and bad fashion. My mum loves it of course. Her favourite period of research.' He smiled at Kik the Assassin's expression. 'Yup, she really is a proper archaeologist.'

Kik the Assassin shrugged again. 'Then I'm glad she likes this time period, because you're all stuck here now.' She activated the device in her hand, screamed and dropped unconscious as a fairly hefty voltage shot through her body.

'Not a keycoder,' he muttered to her. 'Another device I invented to capture idiots on Legion who think like you did. Oh, and another thing you didn't realise about me,' he said bending down towards her, 'is that my Killoran heritage means I'm about three times stronger than a human my age and height.' Effortlessly he picked the assassin up and flung her body over his shoulder.

He sheathed, and thus hid, each of his weapons and devices except his Legion pistol. That he simply carried.

He looked down at Senior Sergeant Rhodes as he

stepped over his body. 'Sorry Sergeant,' he said. 'You are going to wake up in about twenty minutes, along with everyone else in here. Alive. But you are going to spend most of your day in the toilet being very ill. My little neuro-stunners are designed to scramble your synapses, giving you extreme vertigo. Still, better than killing you all, I guess.'

With Kik the Assassin unconscious over his left shoulder, Peter wound his way around the devastated police station, and pushed open the glass front door.

Thirty armed SPG officers raised their guns, clicking off the safety catches audibly, all aiming at Peter from behind cars and armoured trucks.

'Oh, great,' Peter said and looked into the night sky. 'Mum? Jack? Ruth? Anyone, some help please?'

At which point, Sydney suffered another seizure, and all hell broke loose.

'Now, Doctor, did you say Professor Horace Jaanson?'

The Doctor was talking to Keri Pakhar on Legion over speakerphone. Bernice could hear clearly because the smartphone was on the hotel room floor, and the Doctor was pacing around it, thinking.

'We did,' he said.

'Interesting man,' Keri said. 'I've been researching him.'

'Interesting is one word for him,' Bernice conceded. 'Arrogant, idiotic, egomaniac, ignorant – did I say idiotic?'

'You did,' Keri said. 'But here's the interesting thing. Pretty much everything we know about the Ancients of the

Universe does actually come from his family. All of them. Going right back to when GalWiki started. Horace might well be a numpty riding on his forebears' reputation, but without them, a lot of what we know about time-travel theory (Time Lords excepted, Doctor) would be gibberish. He's the latest in a long line of important scientists.'

The Doctor nodded. 'I knew the name was familiar. Wasn't one of his maternal side responsible for proving the symbiotic link between the Time Squids of the Lower Vortex and the Crinis? I met a Crinis once – not fun.'

Keri just carried on. 'So the Jaanson family speculated that, when the Ancients of the Universe did their bunk and vamoosed, various worlds that had been touched by their technology were left with guardians.'

Bernice grabbed the Doctor's sleeve. 'That man. Lue?'

The Doctor nodded. 'Could be. He certainly knew more than he was letting on – and he exists in more than one time zone here on Earth.'

'Well, here's another, important thing about the Pyramid Eternia and why you need to get it off Earth urgently,' Keri said.

'Yes?' the Doctor prompted. Then realised the phone was not responding. He turned back to look at it – only to find it smashed into lots of pieces by Cyrrus Globb's big shoes.

Bernice was on her knees, arms behind her head. 'Wherever we go together, Doctor,' she was saying, 'there's always some mook with a gun pointing it in our faces, shouting and spitting and being incoherent with rage.'

Which pretty much summed up Professor Horace Jaanson at that moment, although the gun was in Cyrrus Globb's hand, and he wasn't upset at all. He seemed to be rather enjoying all this.

'Stupid con artists,' Jaanson was saying.

Globb let out a laugh that sounded not only like he didn't laugh very often, but that it was coming from a very deep pit that didn't encourage laughter because the noise it made was a bit terrifying. 'They're no con artists,' he finally said.

'Are too,' said Bernice.

'Are not,' responded Globb. 'I've been around, lady. Kik the Assassin and I twigged ages ago that you were playing us.'

'We were?' asked the Doctor.

'They were?' asked Jaanson. 'They seemed pretty convincing to me.'

'Makes you a perfect mark, then.' Globb looked at Bernice. 'Tell me some famous cons you've pulled off.'

'Doc's the leader, he'll list them. He's a long-con expert.'

The Doctor gave Bernice a look that suggested strangling her was pretty high on his list of priorities, before smiling at Globb. 'Did you hear about the guy who managed to sell the Sydney Opera House to five different people, until the cops got wind of it?'

'That wasn't you.'

'Might have been. I'm not saying. You might be a cop.'

'I'm not a cop, I'm a conman from the fifty-first century. And are you saying that was you?'

'Could have been.'

'Was it?'

'Yes,' lied the Doctor.

Globb snorted. 'You are a really terrible liar, "Doc". Now, what are you doing here?'

'See?' the Doctor looked at Bernice. 'Everyone asks it eventually.'

'Ever heard of the great Kirrin / Barnard conundrum?' Bernice asked Jaanson and Globb. 'You must have encountered it, Professor. Being so smart and all that.'

For a moment Horace Jaanson looked confused, caught Globb's eye, and swallowed. Hard. 'Of course I have, it postulates that, umm…'

'You're as bad at lying as the others, Prof,' Globb said with a dark smile. 'I really don't like liars. I'm not listening to any more twaddle.'

'Then listen to this, Mr Globb,' the Doctor said, standing up, pushing the gun away. 'Listen carefully. You are not from the twenty-first century but you are human, so you can't stay here. I suspect that's true of the Professor, too. If we don't get the Glamour back to that pyramid, find a way in and get it off this world and back to Aztec Moon, this planet will explode.'

'So?'

'So your ancestors will cease to exist. So will you. Just. Like. This.' He clicked his fingers. 'Gone in a big bang.'

'He's lying,' Jaanson said.

Globb stared into the Doctor's eyes, and then nodded. 'Nah, he's not. He's on the level.' He looked at Jaanson.

'This was fun while it lasted, but I don't want to die here and now.'

For the first time in his life, Horace Jaanson ignored the bullies and the cleverer people and the ones who said they knew better, and he snatched the gun out of Globb's fat, sweaty hand.

He aimed it at all three of them. 'I want the Glamour. The Ancients of the Universe, that pyramid and all their secrets are mine. I have devoted my life to those secrets and I won't be denied.'

He started to squeeze the trigger.

It was 22 December 2015, and Mr Thomas Gordon Taylor was not having a great night. He had returned home to discover that the Rabbitohs had lost and his daughter had scratched his wife's car with her bicycle. To top it all off, at twenty past two in the morning he'd been telephoned and told that the Power Station's alarms had all gone off.

According to his security teams, someone had stolen the weird rock his parents had told him was so important. To be honest, Mr Taylor wasn't too upset by this. OK, so it had been in his family for nearly one hundred years, but he didn't much like it, and his father and grandfather had always been a bit cagey as to how Great Grandad Tomas had got it. There were all sorts of rumours and stories about Nazi sympathisers, Hitler, the occult and the fact that Great Grandma had disappeared overnight. Mr Taylor didn't want to look too deeply into his family history. As a result, the stupid Glamour rock thing had only been in the museum because it was in various wills – an instruction that it had to be for ever and ever. Somehow the news that it had been nicked made Mr Taylor very happy.

Maybe now he could shrug off the ghosts and debts of his ancestors and sell the stupid museum and move to the Gold Coast.

Truth was, after a really bad day, he was now having a good night. He settled back to sleep, having told his staff to coordinate with the police and he'd be in work in the morning to sort things out.

He was just dozing off, when he and his wife fell out of bed as an earthquake shook Sydney badly.

Very badly indeed.

12
Burning the Ground

The night sky in Sydney was cool and refreshing. Peaceful and serene. Beautiful even. Normally. This particular evening however, it was anything but.

The skies were red with flame, volcanoes that had previously been flat land, were wrenched towards the heavens, drenching the city in volcanic lava, choking it with burning ash.

The Doctor stood outside their hotel and looked upwards. It was like Pompeii, Montserrat and Atlantis all in one. He grabbed Bernice's hand. 'We have to get to the pyramid. Where're Jack and the others?'

'I don't know,' Bernice yelled over the noise of people screaming, car horns and other terrible sounds that depicted a city about to die. 'The Bluetooth isn't working.'

'How clever are they?'

'Very,' she said instantly. 'The cleverest people I know.'

'Then hopefully they'll head for the Pyramid Eternia. Come on!'

'What about Globb and the Professor?'

The Doctor looked back. Globb was striding along, his enormous bulk pouring sweat in the heat, but his face showed his determination not to be left behind. In one hand he dragged the Professor, in the other he carried his gun, which he'd retrieved when the earthquake threw Jaanson off his feet. He'd been all for throwing Jaanson into the maw of death that surrounded them, but the Doctor had reminded him that, as they were out of time, displaced chronologically, if the Professor died here before he was ever born, it might cause a few problems with the Web of Time. Total nonsense of course, but in the literal heat of the moment, Globb bought into it.

The Doctor carried the rock.

'We're about two miles from the Harbour Bridge,' Bernice shouted. 'I'm not sure we'll make it!'

All around them, chaos literally erupted as the city convulsed and cracked open. Whole buildings, whole areas sunk instantly into the lava, everything and everyone burned to a crisp in seconds.

Focusing on getting to the Pyramid Eternia so all this could be put right, the Doctor spied a white van nearby. 'Get in,' he yelled.

Bernice got into the driving seat as Globb yanked the rear doors completely away and threw the Professor then himself into the back. Bernice ripped under the steering column until she could hotwire the engine and it roared into life.

'Who taught you that?' the Doctor said as he clambered in beside her.

'Mutual friend,' she said back. 'I call it Ace-ing the engine!' As they moved forward, Bernice looked at the Doctor. 'I don't recall Sydney being destroyed in 2015.'

'It wasn't. But it could be. You know how history likes to reinvent itself. Oh and if you could avoid hitting things, that'd be good.'

Bernice clipped a bin on a kerb as she roared down George Street towards the Harbour.

The Doctor glanced into the wing mirror and watched in horrified fascination as the road and buildings behind them sank into flame.

'I don't think you need to worry about the speed limit, Benny,' he shouted over all the noise from outside.

Another car careering towards them had to swerve and go left.

'That's not good,' Bernice yelled.

'Why not?' growled Globb.

'Because he was driving away from where we need to go which suggests to me that maybe it's already gone. Poof. Up in smoke.'

'I smell burning,' Horace Jaanson whined.

'It's the tyres,' Bernice said. 'We are actually on fire.'

The Doctor opened his door to look at the tyres. Sure enough, tiny flames sparkled amidst the smoke. 'They're melting into the tarmac,' he reported.

'If it ignites the fuel, we're dead,' Bernice said matter-of-factly. 'We've not got much further to go. Do we risk blowing up or risk getting out, running and burning our feet off?'

'Drive!' all three men yelled.

Bernice drove.

When the armed policemen had fallen over, Peter Guy Summerfield had momentarily considered running. But these guys would be better than the normal cops in the station. They were trained for fast reaction and it only took one of them to shoot him dead.

So he stood his ground.

Some of the team staggered to their feet, when a second, larger shake occurred, followed by a noise of a kind Peter had never heard before.

It was like the whole planet had felt this tremor and was screaming out in pain. Or rage. It was an awful, primal noise that frightened him to his very core and, for the first time in his life, Peter was frozen by indecision.

Decision, however, was made when he felt himself scooped up and almost thrown onto the flat roof of the police station, the unconscious Kik the Assassin rolling away from him. She rolled to Ruth's feet, and Peter realised his rescuer was Jack, leaping as he always did so well.

Unaccustomed as he was to gratuitous displays of emotion, Peter hugged Jack, whispering 'Thank you' over and over again.

Then the lava erupted. Peter risked a glance back down, but there was nothing left of any of the people down there, flash fried in a split second. Lava was raining down onto the steps of the station.

'This roof isn't safe,' Ruth said.

'Where to?' asked Peter. 'The hotel?'

'No,' Jack said quietly. 'I think we should head to the pyramid – that's where the Doctor and Benny will go eventually.'

Peter again scooped up Kik the Assassin, but Jack was torn. Of course, he could only carry one person at a time. The pyramid was only maybe a minute away if he jumped from building to building and then down onto the parkland beneath the Bridge.

Peter smiled at them both. 'Take Ruth, I'll be safe here,' he lied.

Jack looked at him. 'Anything happens to you, Benny'll kill me. Slowly. Don't go away or try anything brave. Or stupid.' Then he and Ruth were gone.

Peter looked down again and felt the whole station drop slightly as it started to sink. He looked ahead – the water that surrounded Sydney's collapsing CBD was steaming and with a colossal crash, the Harbour Bridge itself broke in two, the north end dropping into the boiling waterway.

All he could see for miles now was red lava consuming buildings as it roared down from volcanic geysers and he could only imagine that the death toll was going to be, well, indescribable.

All those poor people.

As he thought on this, Peter was aware he was being watched from down below. Not by a policeman but by a civilian – a dark man in a white shirt and chinos. He seemed to just stare at Peter for a second then gave him a ridiculously exaggerated thumbs up, turned and walked into the heat haze and vanished. Peter wanted to call out to him for some reason and he opened his mouth to do so.

At which point he and his unconscious charge were yanked high into the air by the returning Jack, who smiled reassuringly as he leapt them to safety.

'Hey, Petey, miss me?'

As Sydney died around them, the Doctor, Bernice, Ruth, Cyrrus Globb and Horace Jaanson stood at the side of Circular Quay, wondering how to get to the Pyramid Eternia without being broiled.

Then they realised the obvious answer.

Jack flew through the air after one last bouncy leap and deposited Peter and the now awakened Kik the Assassin on a ledge by the doorway.

He then bounded back, grabbed Ruth, and took her to safety. Then the Doctor, Bernice, Jaanson... and then he came back for Globb.

The two men stared at each other.

'Exhausted?' asked Globb.

'Hell, yeah,' said Jack. 'This isn't my natural choice for getting people from A to B.'

Globb looked at his own bulky body, then back at Jack. Then they both looked at the dead city, as even the Opera House blazed in the night sky before it too sank in on itself. 'D'you think anyone got out?'

'In the suburbs? Probably. But here, at ground zero? Not a chance.'

'If I go down with the city,' Globb said, 'they'll never find my body. I'll never even be some weird skeletal anomaly for your Professor Summerfield to discover in a thousand years. I'll just be ash.'

'I'm not leaving you,' Jack said. 'I don't like you one little bit, but as a particular hero of mine once said, "Ohana: nobody gets left behind or forgotten." Now come on.'

With an almighty effort, Jack grabbed Cyrrus Globb and jumped as high and far as he could. A second later, both men plummeted towards the boiling, scalding water, well short of the Pyramid Eternia.

'No!' screamed Ruth from the pyramid ledge. Peter pulled her back to stop her from almost falling in too.

Faster than anyone could really see, Bernice threw herself off the pyramid towards the dropping duo, reaching for them with one hand, reaching backwards with the other, shooting a grappling hook back to the pyramid.

The Doctor grabbed the cable once it embedded itself in the wall of the structure, holding it taut as Bernice swung round, grabbing Jack's left ankle and pulling his momentum around. Instead of the water, Jack, Bernice and Globb slammed into the pyramid, further down.

Globb looked at both Jack and Bernice, and then up at the Doctor, still holding the cable tightly, now helped by Peter and Ruth and Kik the Assassin.

'Thank you,' he growled, and stared to climb upwards.

Bernice hugged Jack. 'You OK?'

'No,' he muttered. 'Don't tell Ruth but I think I just dislocated my shoulder and left hip.'

'Why don't you want her to know?'

'Because I can't have a wedding on crutches and in plaster.'

Bernice helped him back up, smiling in sympathy as he winced in pain.

Horace Jaanson was staring at the huge door to the Pyramid Eternia, just as he had when this had all begun on Aztec Moon. 'How do we get in?'

Bernice took the rock from the Doctor. 'Open Sesame,' she said, again echoing what she had done on Aztec Moon.

And the door swung open.

The Doctor ushered everyone inside, one by one. Just as he was about to go in, he looked back at what little remained of the great city of Sydney, and realised that standing, unfazed by the flame and smoke and utter devastation, was a man. In a white shirt.

'Lue?'

He waved some ash out of his face, blown there on a sudden wind. When it was gone, the Indigenous man was gone too.

Inside the Pyramid Eternia, everything was calm, as if it was in a different place altogether.

'Like the inside of the TARDIS,' Bernice muttered as they walked ahead.

Finally they reached the altar area where Benny had seen future reflections of herself, Peter, Jack and Ruth. This time there was no Glamour / lodestone / key, whatever the rock was truly called. Instead, a beam of pulsating energy arced upwards, like a series of concentric Jacob's Ladder discs of electricity.

'What's going on?' Horace Jaanson asked as they made their way safely down to the altar – no jumping this time, just a long hard climb down.

'This?' The Doctor threw an arm up at the energy around them. 'This Professor Horace Jaanson of the fifty-first century, is the end of the universe, courtesy of the Ancients of the Universe. And it's pretty much all your fault, because you just couldn't leave it alone, could you?' The Doctor smiled. 'And now it's up to me to save everything. Again.'

13
Last Man Standing

'Signals,' the Doctor said. 'They're just like TV signals, beamed out into space, going nowhere but picked up. By someone. And deciphered.'

'Or not,' Bernice added. 'Half the time the guys that find this stuff are watching an episode of *Top Gear* and assume it's a comedy show about three bumbling mechanics building stupid methods of transport.'

'It isn't?' asked Jack.

'It isn't,' Bernice confirmed.

'But that one with the bathtub…'

'That's *Last of the Summer Wine*.'

'Oh.' Jack frowned. 'What's the difference again?'

'Aaanyway,' the Doctor continued, smiling at Jaanson, 'the last time this happened, these Ancients of yours sent out their signal. When no one replied, they rather gave up.'

'Went out on a binge,' Bernice added helpfully.

Jaanson looked like someone had just defiled his personal Holy Grail. 'The Ancients are sublime! You cannot malign them in this way.'

'I think she can,' the Doctor said.

'I think she did,' Peter added.

'Absolutely,' Bernice said, tapping the Glamour, or lodestone or whatever it really was. 'This little doohickey is a transmitter trigger, shooting those signals out. Except they're not really TV signals. More like big-nasty-let's-change-the-matter-of-the-universe signals,' she added.

'And that is not good news.' The Doctor threw an arm around Jaanson's shoulders. 'You do see that, don't you, Professor?'

'Not really, no.'

'Your life's work has been not so much uncovering a potential gateway to glory and Valhalla or Avalon or Nirvana or the Axis Mundi or Paradise or even Sto'Vo'Kor. No, effectively all you've dedicated yourself to doing is finding the one switch for a big transmitter that, when it was switched on, would broadcast a pulse not just through space but through time as well, in every direction, and that ultimately would change the history of everything. And because it would go in every direction, everything would be in flux. No sooner would history be rewritten in the past than it would be rewritten in the future, which in turn would require a rewrite in the past, which would trigger a rewrite in the present and so on and so on. Are you following this?'

'Not really,' muttered Jaanson.

'Basically, you would turn off the universe. Oh, it'd take a few millennia as the reshaping, rewriting and remapping crawled along the Web of Time, but you wouldn't be aware of that because you'd be you one minute, a dog the next, a grain of sand the next, a beetle for maybe a second longer and so on. Eventually, the signal would go back to either the Big Bang or forward to the Heat Death of the Universe and rewrite those and it's all over. Just a big void of perpetually imploding and exploding chronon energy that finally wipes itself out.' The Doctor smiled. 'Simple, yes?'

Standing slightly away from the group, Kik the Assassin put a hand on Peter's shoulder. 'In a changed reality, perhaps you could love me?'

Peter smiled at her. 'But it would only be for less than a heartbeat.'

'Ah, but what an exhilarating, amazing heartbeat that would be.'

Peter shook his head. 'I still wouldn't be worth it.'

'You would,' Kik the Assassin continued. 'Believe me, I know myself even if you don't know yourself. It would be the most wonderful heartbeat in the history of creation.'

'I'm sorry,' Peter said, 'that I can't give you what you want. I wish I could. But I can't.'

Kik the Assassin nodded. 'I understand. I shall never truly accept it, but I do understand why it can never be.'

The Doctor was standing slightly back from the Glamour, now in its rightful position on the altar, and took out his sonic screwdriver. 'I don't think this is really going to do much, but perhaps it'll scramble the thing enough that I can buy some time to work out how to really shut it down.'

'How?' asked Ruth.

'I'm a Time Lord,' the Doctor said.

'And that means what in this situation?' asked Jack, not unreasonably.

'It means that there are many chronon-energy-based events that I can withstand better than most. Time schisms, time eddies, time distorts, time fields, time ruptures, time quakes...'

'Cakes? What's a time cake?' Jack laughed.

'He said "quake", nitwit,' Ruth said, nudging him in the ribs.

'Not "time cake"? I'd love to eat time cake,' Jack replied.

The Doctor sighed dramatically. 'As I was saying, although not for long and not always as precisely as I'd like, as a Time Lord I can withstand the changes in time that surround such events for a while. A bit. Longer than any of you lot can, anyway. So I suggest that Benny moves you all back to safety while I focus on shutting this thing down.'

Out of the corner of his eye, Peter saw something. He tried to draw his gun but he wasn't fast enough. Nor did his yell propel the Doctor or Bernice into action quickly enough.

What he saw was Professor Jaanson throwing himself at the Glamour. With a cry of 'No, you can't do this,' the man slammed his fists down, hitting, punching and swiping everything at once.

The Doctor had a split second to recall what he and Bernice had seen back in Australia in 1934, when Tomas

Schneidter's men had vanished as the universe began rewriting itself. But, cruel as it was to think, those people had been insignificant in the grand scheme of things. Here and now, this was different because Horace Jaanson's entire heritage had probably been created purely to serve the Ancients. Here, Jaanson was right at the epicentre of it all, and he winked out of existence.

At exactly that nanosecond, Professor Jaanson's entire family tree was also erased – the human cell that brought his first ancestor into being at the dawn of time was simply never created. That cell of amino acids and DNA just became another grain of sand. All the Jaansons throughout time winked out of existence and, as the universe tried to accommodate this change and rewrite itself, all the things touched by the Jaansons in whatever major or minor way rewrote themselves. And all the things that connected with those things rewrote themselves too, backwards and forwards in time. As Jaanson's parents vanished, so did Jaanson's own potential offspring.

Time, in both directions, and quite a few sideways 'what if' ones, just ceased to happen.

And as that series of time echoes dissipated, so others that fell into their place, like water filling a hole on a beach, ceased to exist too. And the more time and the universe tried to fill those holes, the more things were rewritten or ceased to be…

In Marbella, a barman in 1964 became a lump of coal…

In fourteenth-century Turkey, a sword became a blade of grass…

In thirty-first-century Swansea, a wedding party all turned into dinosaurs before turning into amoebas before becoming bananas before becoming…

A gumblejack swimming in the seas of Medazzaland turned into a hamster and drowned; the air escaping its lungs became fire; the smoke became granite, the tiny flakes becoming a wooden chair…

A human woman and a Martian warrior celebrating their eighteenth wedding anniversary with their three children posed for a holovid when they all became two-dimensional beings that suffocated in three-dimensional winds…

On Legion, Keri the Pakhar saw her glass of water become the molten core of a planet before she was vaporised…

The twin planets of Romulus and Remus became respectively solid gold and solid glass, the sudden change in density disrupting their solar system, causing a black hole to open up. As it began sucking everything into itself, the black hole became a small furry rabbit-like creature, unable to exist in the vacuum of space, so it exploded…

Mr Thomas Gordon Taylor hid under his bed with his wife

and daughter, wondering how they were going to survive the destruction of Sydney as his entire ancestry became cockroaches…

The Big Bang fizzled like a damp firework then blinked out…

The Heat Death of the Universe went cold and, as time fractured backwards from that, it met fractured time coming forward from the lack of Big Bang – time hit time and just ceased…

At the eye of this storm, the Doctor felt time die and pushed himself forward, exactly as he had just told his friends he could. He could see Kik the Assassin and Cyrrus Globb frozen in a beat of time, unable to move, unaware that they couldn't, oblivious to the fate that would hit them in a microsecond or a decade, depending how fast the Ancients' power affected the localised area. He reached for the controls that had destroyed Jaanson. As he stretched and stretched, they seemed to be an infinity away and yet beneath his hand at the same time.

He became aware of another hand on his, pushing him forward. In the slowest of slow motions, he managed to turn his head. In his mind he was screaming, 'What are you doing? And how?' but of course time didn't allow those thoughts to reach the physical plane of his mouth. Instead he allowed Professor Bernice Summerfield to add her strength to his.

Then there was more. Ruth and Jack, each pushing Bernice's hand firmly against the Doctor's. They had to know what was going to happen – they weren't Time Lords, they weren't protected.

Then there was Peter, also grasping his mother's hand, his strength a real asset. But they were going to die, they were going to have never existed. Everything they had done, every scheme, every adventure, every wrong they had righted would be unravelled.

Not that it would matter to Time. Because if the Doctor could stop the Ancients' power, everything should snap back into place. He could hear the voice of his old tutor at the Academy on Gallifrey…

'What are the time streams of ephemeral beings when weighed against universal, multiversal cataclysm? Sacrifices must be made.'

For a brief second, as all their hands hit the Ancients' device, there was utter calm. Utter serenity.

'How are you doing this?' the Doctor asked.

Bernice grinned. 'All those years travelling with you, years using Time Rings, years frankly just messing around with causality – it's affected me, too, made me immune to Time, to some extent. Why do you think I age so slowly? And gracefully, I know you're thinking gracefully.' She smiled. 'And if all that extra juice, all that stored-up chronon energy means I have to sacrifice it to save a universe, hell, Doctor, I can't say it hasn't been fun.'

Ruth was staring at Jack. 'I do love you, you know. And if I'm going to die here, dying with you beside me makes me happy, not sad.'

Before Jack could reply, Peter just swore. 'You're making a little bit of sick creep into my mouth.'

Then they were gone – a brief flash of white, and Ruth, Jack and Peter were not even memories. The Doctor looked at Bernice. Kind, clever, witty (caustically so at times) and strong Bernice Summerfield. And she smiled at him, knowing her time was over. And the Doctor watched as her face blurred and changed. And he was facing Clara Oswald. Who smiled, blurred and became Amy Pond. Who blurred and became Rory Williams, then River Song, then Wilfred Mott then Donna Noble, Martha Jones, Jack Harkness, Mickey Smith, Rose Tyler, Cinder, Molly O'Sullivan, Tamsin Drew, Lucie Miller, C'rizz, Charlotte Pollard, Samson Griffin, Gemma Griffin, Mary Shelley, Grace Holloway, Ace McShane, Hex, Mel Bush, Evelyn Smythe and so many others... Face after face after face, his past companions swam into existence and out again, getting faster and faster so that he couldn't discern them until, with a final flash, there was one face. Small, dark-haired, elfin featured, a big grin on her face.

'You came back after all, Grandfather,' she said.

Then she too was gone.

And the Doctor was... elsewhere.

It was dark, so very dark, no matter how hard he tried, he just couldn't adjust. But he knew, somehow, that he hadn't gone blind, it really was just too dark to see anything.

After a few seconds that might have been minutes or hours or days – he had no way of telling because he had no real sense of self other than his own mind telling him this was real, this was happening, this was –

Light. Something shimmering towards him; high, high up. He let his eyes focus on it, letting it all come into full vision. When it did, he understood what he was witness to.

There were three beings before him, and many others further off, he was sure of that, although he couldn't actually discern anything of them.

In fact he couldn't really discern those close to him. They had more a suggestion of shape, of physicality, of being rather than actually being there.

'Hullo,' he said, surprised but pleased that his voice worked.

There was silence. Then a voice echoed back 'Hullo', but not in mimicry.

'I'm the Doctor. Where am I?'

'I'm the Doctor. Where am I?'

'Last time this happened to me, people repeating my words, it really didn't go very well for me, so if we could avoid all that. I'm guessing that you are trying to translate my speech, understand my language. So maybe if I keep talking, you'll just let me know when you're done, and that way I'll know when to shut up, because it is very exhausting doing this. I mean, have you any idea just how exhausting it is talking into a void and—'

'You are the Doctor. Welcome, Time Lord. That is a vast and powerful domain to claim lordship over.'

The Doctor smiled wryly. 'Some would say differently.'

'Some would be wrong. Time is everything. Time is all. Without Time, nothing can exist, no flow, no flux. Destruction.'

A little light glowed off to the right and the Doctor could see some shapes. It was Bernice and her friends, but they were in slightly different clothes. Globb, Kik the Assassin, Jaanson and some military types were there too – all of them, frozen in a moment of time.

'They disturbed us,' said the voice by way of explanation.

The Doctor tried to see the speaker, looking beyond the shapes closest to him, but he couldn't. It was as if reality shifted to accommodate his attempts, ensuring he could never truly feel comfortable.

'I take it you are the Ancients?'

'To you, that may be how we are defined. To ourselves, we cannot be defined for we are ageless, infinite, eternal, forever—'

'Well, before you get all thesaurus-y on me, let's just accept that's who you are to me, OK? Good. Now then, I have to ask before we go any further – because a lot has happened and people have died trying to find this out – where the hell have you been?'

The Doctor was suddenly in yet another place. A vast alien arena, a thousand eyes watching events at the centre. Two vast beings from different worlds, fighting to the death.

He looked around. The crowd was made up of aliens from a hundred different worlds, cheering, gambling, being savage. Then his eyes focused on what it was he was looking for. Sort of. Across the auditorium was a blur, like watching someone interviewed on television but, because they're wearing a T-shirt or baseball cap with a logo on it, the TV have to blur it out, pixelate it to a soft mass of colour. That was what the Ancients were to the Doctor here. Unfocused blurs. But he could tell from the way they were positioned, they weren't joining in. They were bored.

The arena melted around him and he was on a spaceship in the throes of war, a dozen ships firing upon him. Around him, the Federality of Bandril were taking hit after hit. A couple of bridge officers weren't Bandrils, they were blurred, unfocused Ancients again, but clearly the Bandrils didn't see them as anything unusual.

Realty warped once more. The Doctor was in a night-time street, lots of noise, raucous merry making. Humans, mostly male, were in the streets and open-fronted bars, singing and yelling and occasionally fighting or throwing up. Relentless house music pumped from each bar, competing with the other bars trying to drown them out – it was a dreadful, nightmarish world.

'Oh god, I'm in Ibiza,' the Doctor muttered.

He looked across at one bar and sure enough, making as much noise as the humans, towering above them, blurred as always were the Ancients, knocking back mojitos and piña coladas by the dozen.

He understood. The Ancients had, as always rumoured, gone out into the universe in disguise and partied. Then, bored of that, got into fights. Then, bored of that, sat and watched the universe go by. Then, bored of that…

'We created this null space in which we could sleep. Rest. Chill out, man.'

The dark room was suddenly illuminated by soft shapes floating around the walls, like reflected globs of gel from lava lamps. Soft ambient music started up and the Doctor could see scatter cushions, bean bags and incense burners.

'Ah the chill-out zone of Lymnos,' he nodded appreciatively. 'I brought Jamie and Zoe here once. Tried to explain the concept of relaxation and switching your mind off to the world to Zoe. She never got it, you know.'

'Why are you here, Doctor?'

'Tell me where we really are and I promise to answer that.'

The blackness returned. 'We are in our end-place, one microsecond beyond the destruction of time and space, beyond the collapse of the multiverse, beyond the absence of all.'

'Well, that explains why I managed to track you down, then. Because you're no longer in any of those things.'

'Explain?'

'You left a device behind, on Aztec Moon. A portal to this place. You assumed no one would find it, access it, use it.'

'The pyramid is impenetrable.'

'Hullo, I'm right here. If it was impenetrable, how did I get here?'

'Why did you access it?'

'I didn't. Others did. Foolish beings who were only interested in personal glory and, well, curiosity. The last bit I get, I've been guilty of that myself once or twice or sixty-eight times. But I digress! Your pyramid was accessed, moved and therefore weakened.'

'To be used successfully, it needed the trigger device. We did not leave that in the pyramid on – what did you call it? Aztec Moon.'

'No. No, you didn't. You took it with you, yes?'

'Indeed.'

'And you planned to hang on to it, making sure no one could ever use the power within the Pyramid.'

'Indeed.'

'So what happened to it?'

'We do not understand the question.'

'Yes, you do. You lost it, didn't you?'

'It became separated from us.'

'Lost it.'

'It was misplaced in time.'

'Looooost it.'

'It became disconjoined.'

'Oh, do stop all this nonsense. You lost it fair and square. Want to know where?'

'Yes.'

'Then read my mind.' And the Doctor closed his eyes. Then as he felt a brush of air on his cheek he smiled and opened them. 'Welcome to Sydney's Blue Mountains,' he breathed. 'One of the most beautiful places on planet Earth.'

He was aware that he was surrounded by a large number of blurred unfocused Ancients. Two, ten, a hundred? Who knew?

'It's 36,000 BC, give or take a century or ten. Look over there.' He pointed to a rock formation to the north. Four menhir-shaped rocks pointed up into the sky, like prongs on a fork. 'Created by erosion from the wind, the rain, all the elements of this primordial world. If you stare into the bushland below, you might find examples of this country's settlers, the Gundungurra as they'll eventually be called. And they are busy creating legends. Right now they are deciding if those are entombed people or great beasts or any number of other things. But any second now, their worldview is going to be changed because of you. Look.'

The Doctor pointed to the sky and, sure enough, through the clouds, three blurred shapes, three Ancients, like a three-pointed star, dropped towards Earth.

'Skydiving. One of your many pastimes, no doubt. "Hey, guys, I'm bored. Let's go skydive a primitive world, see if we can be mistaken for gods, or monsters or anything to dull the unending tedium of eternity."' The Doctor shrugged. 'I mean, that might not be word for word what they said, but I bet I'm pretty damn close. And then, there's a problem.'

The skydiving blurs separated, and went in different directions, one of which included straight down. The blurred Ancient smashed into the menhir-shaped rock formation, shattering and slicing away the outermost. The other two blurs joined their compatriot and quickly shot back up into the sky, leaving the mountains forever changed.

'And somewhere, down there, whichever of you it was, had keepership of the trigger device to the pyramid on Aztec Moon and you dropped it.'

The Doctor realised he was no longer alone. Beside him was Lue. He cast his head down.

'I failed,' he said simply.

'You did,' said the Doctor. 'And as the centuries rolled by, it sank deeper into the base of the mountain until sometime around the 1930s, when some idiot decided to invent a backstory to those rocks, which had become called the Three Sisters, and treasure seekers from across the southern hemisphere came to dig, root around and generally mess with the landscapes here. Oh, in time it became a marvellous tourist spot, protected and honoured for both the Australian people and the Gundungurra people.'

The air shimmered around them all and the whole Blue Mountain area was now swarming with humans.

The Doctor pointed as he said, 'I'm getting the hang of all this. Now look, down there: Tomas G. Schneidter, Bavarian archaeologist. He found your trigger. He touched it. It did something to his mind because he was the first non-Ancient in history to touch the device. He called it the Glamour. It cost him dearly and he was forced to become a renegade from his homeland, lost his wife and lived out the remainder of his life in an asylum. The Glamour was sent, by his grandson's son, to a museum in

Sydney. And there it stayed under his family's protection for decades. They didn't know why they had to protect it but, on some level, some subconscious level, it spoke to Schneidter, and his descendants, the Taylors as they are now, have looked after it for you ever since.'

'That was good of them.' Lue looked up at the Doctor ,and his features blurred as he became what he truly was – one of the Ancients of the Universe. He disappeared, joining his out-of-focus fellow Ancients... somewhere else.

The Doctor wasn't surprised. 'Yes, yes it was very good of them. Until some idiot from three thousand years in the future wandered into your now unguarded pyramid and activated it, and it promptly decided to seek out its missing component. And, well – here we are.'

Then the Doctor was back in the Ancients' darkness.

'And now it has been activated, the universe is gone, time erased, and I'm here because it's the only place left to go.'

'So what?'

'So what?? So, put it right. Turn it off, reverse the polarity of its neutron flow, turn it off and turn it back on again, I don't know. But you have to resolve this.'

'Why?'

'Because I'm already the last of the Time Lords, I really don't want to be the last of everything ever.'

'That is of no interest to us.'

'Then think on this. When all that's left is you in this little pocket existence, one heartbeat out of sync with reality, one day you might want to step back outside, see, feel, breathe again. One day you might want to see the skies, swim in the seas. You might even want to have a night at Es Paradis back on Ibiza as you like pyramids so much. But you will be unable to do any of that, for eternity, if you don't take control of your equipment and step back into the real worlds.'

'It may be too late. You say the universe is gone.'

'I'm a Time Lord. You're the Ancients. You brought me here. You seriously think that together we can't sort this out?'

'Yes.'

'Oh. Well, that's a bit negative. How about you ask yourselves what you have to lose by trying?'

'Mojitos,' a new Ancient voice said. 'I liked those.'

'I liked the wars.' Another new voice.

'I enjoyed painting the trees and flowers.'

'I like the music of the spheres.'

'I just want to go home again.'

And the voices stopped.

And the Doctor waited.

And the Ancients blurred out of existence.

And the Doctor was in darkness again.

And…

The Doctor was pushing forward. It was like walking through treacle. Or jelly. Or treacle dipped in jelly.

All he could focus on was the hieroglyphs that had destroyed Professor Jaanson. Everyone around him was frozen by the time spillage. Kik the Assassin. Globb. Peter. Ruth. Jack. Even Bernice.

But surely… but last time… but what did 'last time' mean? Had this happened before?

As his hand reached out, ignoring the roar of time, ignoring the destruction of everything he held dear, the Doctor felt a new power behind him. He couldn't turn; he couldn't look. Every fibre of his being wanted to turn, to gaze upon the true face of the Ancients that he now realised were with him.

But he simply couldn't. He had to trust that they were there.

His hand hit the controls. Pushed there by another, dark hand.

The Doctor turned slightly and saw Lue – although his features were still just a blur.

'Told you we'd met again, right?' Lue said. 'And we will again. That will not be… pleasant. It is my job to look after you, Doctor, during something very bad that will happen in your future. I am… sorry.'

The Doctor looked back down at his hand, feeling pressure on it as another blurred hand hit it, pushing against the controls. And another. And another. Five. Ten. Twenty. He gave up trying to count how many blurs passed through his hand and into the trigger, the lodestone, the Glamour, whatever it was called.

Then he felt another hand.

This one he knew by touch.

Bernice Summerfield, fighting through time again.

This time he didn't stop to wonder why or how because his memories were back. He knew he had indeed done this before, just as he knew the Ancients were helping.

There was a massive white flash.

A man in Marbella wasn't a lump of coal.

A fish wasn't a hamster.

Stacey Townsend and Ssard the Ice Warrior celebrated their anniversary on Mars with their kids intact.

The Big Bang happened. The Heat Death of the Universe happened.

In Sydney Harbour, the pyramid, the wrecked bridge and a fairly significant amount of water vanished and reappeared instantaneously on Aztec Moon. The water bled into the cold, red surface and, above the bridge, parts of the planet, undisturbed in millennia, were flung up into the air and floated like rust-coloured boulders around the tops of the pylons. In this reality, nothing yet lived on the planet and so there was no one to see this amazing spectacle.

Just as instantly, the Sydney Harbour Bridge reassembled, fully repaired. Then it, and the water that came with it, were gone, snapped back to Earth like they were on cosmic elastic. History returned to the right path on both planets, although this time the pyramid stayed on Aztec Moon, encased in a mountain that hadn't been there micro-moments previously.

In Sydney, life carried on as before – nothing that had happened would be remembered as more than a bad dream. No one ever talked about the pyramid they dreamed they might have seen for fear they would be considered fools.

Senior Sergeant Rhodes's police station was never attacked. The Arcadia Hotel never had rooms booked by the weirdo Summerfield group. And the Power Station was never burgled, because the Glamour was never there. In its place the curator, Thomas Gordon Taylor, was proud to display, as he always had, an ancient Aboriginal artefact that the eminent archaeologist Tomas G. Schneidter had found in the Blue Mountains in 1934 and which was kept on display with the full support of the Gundungurra. It was a simple painting from thousands of years ago, showing an Indigenous man wearing white hide.

In a Stormcage in the fifty-first century, Kik the Assassin delivered herself and Cyrrus Globb up for re-arrest, aware that only they knew what had transpired.

In 1934, a dark-skinned man in an open-necked white shirt and chinos, smiled and nodded his thanks to something unseen and walked into the rainforests of the Blue Mountains.

*

In the fifty-first century, Colonel Sadkin of the Church of the Papal Mainframe stared as Professor Jaanson and a Talpidian digger tried to protect themselves from the rain.

There was a flash and, for a brief second, he thought he saw the outline of a door on the side of the mountain. He blinked. No one else mentioned it.

'Professor Jaanson,' he grunted. 'I think this mission needs to be aborted before the weather turns.'

Horace Jaanson opened his mouth to argue, then shrugged. 'You're probably right, Colonel. Without a decent archaeologist to help us, I don't think we'll find anything here. I'm beginning to doubt that Aztec Moon is even the right location for the Ancients of the Universe.'

And, much to his satisfaction, Colonel Sadkin and his Clerics were able to pack up and get away from Aztec Moon before the rains took an even worse turn.

The TARDIS was flying through the space-time vortex, the Doctor rushing around from side to side, flipping buttons, punching switches (or maybe it was the other way round, although if that was what he was doing, it probably explained why the TARDIS rarely did as she was meant to). With an almighty flourish, the whole ship lurched on its side and the doors popped open.

A beautiful blue sky could be seen through the doors as the TARDIS hovered somewhere on its side, like an open coffin.

After a second or two, something large and heavy dropped towards the open doors. Beyond that, something larger and heavier struck a mountainside, and the TARDIS was pelted with rocks and rubble. But the only thing that fell into the ship was a small rock with crystal lines running through it.

The Doctor caught it like a rugby ball, allowing its momentum to swirl him round, back towards the TARDIS console, which he thumped. The ship's interior righted itself, and the TARDIS dematerialised from the ancient Australian Blue Mountains area.

The Doctor was back in the dark void. This time he knew what to expect.

As the blurred Ancients loomed up, he held out the trigger device. 'Now no one other than me has ever touched this.'

And it winked out of existence.

'Will they remember, or has time been reset?'

'Nothing involving our technology will have happened. Has happened. Could happen. Did happen. Time has changed; tiny chronological events have been rewritten to alter the histories of those involved with our error. Our mistakes. But no one will ever know.'

Again the Doctor thought back to his tutor at the Academy on Gallifrey. He had always hated the thought that ephemeral lives were unimportant enough to affect the Web of Time. But right now, he had to admit, it was for the best.

'So I am the only one who remembers any of this?'

'You are a Lord of Time. That is your role. However…'

'Yes?'

'There were six other beings at the eye of the time storm. If we erase their participation in bringing you to our attention in the first place, it would create a paradox. Without them, you would not have arrived, changed time and saved the universe, so to erase them would stop that happening. They too will be aware of what they did, if nothing else.'

'Good,' the Doctor said. 'Bernice Summerfield is my friend and I would feel very unhappy if I thought I had somehow stolen part of her experiences and her life.'

'We shall not meet again, Lord of Time. That is as it should be.'

'Will you return to the universe? Return to live, feel, see, experience? Have a mojito?'

But before he got an answer, he was elsewhere.

The smell. The sticky floors. The broken neon sign flickering.

'Oh no,' he muttered. 'The White Rabbit. On Legion. Great.'

14
Pressure Off

'Oh, so you decided to come back, then.'

The Doctor looked at Keri the Pakhar and beeped her twitching nose. 'As if I'd leave you behind on a godforsaken place like Legion.'

'You left me on Tugrah.'

'Ah. well, yes, all right, but—'

'You left me on the Azure Moon of Gald too.'

'That was ages ago. You have a good memory—'

'Then there was that time you left me in jail on Kolpasha.'

'Blimey, you really can hold a grudge, can't—'

'I seem to recall an incident on Nefrin where you said, and I quote: "Keri, I'll be back in five." I, of course, took that to mean minutes. Maybe hours at a push. Not years. Guarding that Eternity Capsule took a lot of time and energy, yeah!'

The Doctor sighed. 'I got held up. There was a planet, an invading horde of Scarrions, an under-trodden village and a party. Well, a lot of parties. Well, it was just one long party really…'

'That lasted five years?'

'I left early. It went on for about eighteen.' The Doctor put a glass of fizzy water in front of her. 'But I'm here now. Ready to take you away from all this.'

Keri pointed at the bar of the White Rabbit. 'You met the guy who used to own this place, yeah?'

The Doctor shook his head.

'You should. You'd like him. Reminds me of you. Duplicitous, underhanded, talks too much about absolutely nothing, wears terrible clothes and flirts outrageously.'

'I don't flirt. I have never flirted. I'm not sure I know how to flirt without making a fool of myself.'

'Another thing in common with him, then.'

Bernice Summerfield and Peter walked over. 'Hey, Keri,' said Bernice. 'Nice to see you again.'

'It's been a long time.' Keri smiled. 'Missed you. Sorry you got lumbered with this old fraud.' She waved towards the Doctor. Then she smiled at Peter. 'Last time I saw you, you were a tiny puppy, yeah?' She looked at Bernice with a querying look on her face.

'Baby,' Bernice said. 'He was a baby.'

'Baby, yes, of course.'

Peter leaned forward and gave Keri a quick kiss then grabbed Bernice's arm. 'Mum, I have to go settle a dispute between Crazy Hank and Toothless Bob over a Land Crow.'

Bernice considered this information. 'You know, I think I'd pay good money to see those two scrap.' She kissed Peter's forehead. 'See you later.'

Peter looked at the Doctor.

'What?' the Time Lord asked. 'What's that look for? I know that look. That's a look that says I've done something wrong. What? What have I done wrong now?'

Peter reached behind the bar and brought out a thin metallic stick, twisted and almost snapped in half.

'Yours, I believe. Apparently, a pretty peeved Kenistrii left it here before heading home.' He slapped it into the Doctor's palm. 'Don't leave advanced Time Lord tech on my planet, thank you.'

The Doctor looked at his broken sonic screwdriver. 'Sorry Peter,' the Doctor heard himself say, like a teenager being told off by an old man, rather than the other way round.

'See you round, Doc,' Peter laughed and headed out of the bar.

'Where are Ruth and Jack?' the Doctor asked. 'I like Ruth and Jack.'

'They're down at my little underground base in the mountains, reprogramming EOIN, the computer that runs the place You'd like him. He never gives anyone any cheek.'

'When's the wedding?' Keri asked. 'I might hang around for the wedding, yeah.'

'I thought you wanted to go home,' exploded the Doctor. 'I mean, you just said—'

'If I relied on you to get me home, or back here for the wedding, we'd end up in the eighty-sixth century or taking a sky train to the Planet of the Hats.'

'Have you been to the Planet of the Hats?' asked Bernice.

'No,' sneered the Doctor. 'There's no such place as the Planet of the Hats.'

Bernice and Keri looked at one another, shocked. 'He's never been to the Planet of the Hats!'

'With the Brown Derbys!'

'And the Stingy Brims!'

'The rebellious Cloche!'

'The warring Homburgs and Pillboxes!'

The Doctor stood up. 'If no one's going to have a sensible conversation…'

'The Planet of the Hats is a real place,' Bernice said seriously.

'It's not.'

'I did a story there during one of their wars,' Keri said. 'I was embedded with the Gainsboroughs. It was quite scary.'

'Hair-raising, even,' Bernice added. She leaned down and hugged Keri. 'Thank you for everything you did for us,' she said.

'Everything I did? I don't know what you're talking about, yeah?'

Bernice looked at the Doctor. 'Keri, too?'

'Everyone other than us, Kik the Assassin and Globb I believe.'

'Well, believe me, it was invaluable,' Bernice said. 'Wasn't it, Doctor?'

'Invaluable. Essential. Very grateful.' He nodded.

'Well, I have no idea what either of you is going on

about, but either way, if Legion will have me,' Keri said, tapping her leg in its cast, 'I think I'll stick around till this repairs itself.'

'Be lovely to have you here. Get the guy who runs this place to give you his spare room. Tell him I insist,' Bernice said.

'I'll do that.'

The Doctor squeezed Keri's shoulder as he started to move away. 'If you're sure?'

'Absolutely. Take care, Doctor. Deep down, you're a good man. If you look hard enough.' She winked. 'But I'm never ice skating with you again, yeah?'

The Doctor allowed Bernice to lead him out of the bar and into the street outside.

Neon signs were reflected in the muddy puddles that were growing larger in the rain.

'You notice how it always rains when we're together,' he said. 'Never met anyone else who I can guarantee no matter what places I go, it'll always be raining with.'

'We need your TARDIS.'

The Doctor looked shocked. 'My TARDIS! It's in Sydney. Hundreds of years ago!'

'No, it's not. It's over there. Believe me, no one else leaves a 1950s police box lying about.'

The Doctor followed her finger. Sure enough, the TARDIS was parked under an awning for a tattoo parlour.

'The Ancients of the Universe must have shot it back here, to its last landing before this all started,' Bernice said.

'How nice of them,' he said. 'Where are we going?'

'More a question of when. Come on.' And Bernice led him inside his ship.

About forty miles north of Legion City was a plateau that few people wanted to visit. Dark, cold and inhospitable it was, of course, exactly where Professor Bernice Summerfield had decided to do a bit of digging.

Jack and Ruth were examining some strata in the rocks about half a mile away.

Peter was in the distance strategically placing some low-level explosives to clear some rubble.

Bernice looked up. She stopped, chewed on her lower lip for a second, then shrugged. 'Hullo,' she said eventually.

'Hullo,' called another Bernice. And next to her, a tall greying man. Somehow, she knew instinctively that it was the Doctor.

'Future-me, or past-me that I've forgotten for some reason?' Bernice called to the newcomers.

'I'm really not sure about this,' the probably Doctor person said.

This other Bernice shushed him. 'Past. Not quite sure how long. Probably breaking the Laws of Time if I tell you. But then casually breaking the Laws of Time is why we're here.'

'Really?'

The Doctor stepped forward. 'Yes. Apparently so. It's why I'm here.'

'I thought he'd add gravitas, you know, make you realise that you need to listen to me. To us.'

Bernice nodded. 'Makes sense I guess. Although this could be a temporal trap.'

'It could be indeed. But let's face it, I've got this far based on instinct. And something about this feels right. Or interesting at the very least.'

'What if I told you, Benny,' the Doctor said, 'that digging here would be catastrophic?'

'I'd say, "Hell, really? Here?" in a pretty sarcastic voice and then say, "But I'm listening" and suggest you carry on.'

Other Bernice stepped forward. 'It's an instruction from you. Future you. *Future*-future-me, in fact. I have to make sure you don't dig anything up here.'

'What sort of anything?'

'That would be telling,' the Doctor said. 'Let's just say something is buried here that needs to stay buried for the sake of the universe.'

'Don't be melodramatic,' Bernice snorted.

'I'm not.' He looked at Other Bernice. 'Do I sound in the slightest bit melodramatic?'

'No, not at all. You just sound dour and Scottish. That's about as far from melodramatic as you can get really.'

'Thank you.' He paused. 'Dour? How am I dour? I'm the very epitome of party spirit.'

'Yeah, if the party is in a funeral home and the spirit is one of the dead. Aaaanyway…' Other Bernice looked back at Bernice. 'You need to pack up, go home, forget this place. Please.'

'Why?' Bernice looked around the plateau. 'It's hardly the most threatening place on Legion. I mean, I've been to

Madame JoJoJos on a Wednesday night. Now, as bars go, that's a scary place!'

'Oh, I know!' Other Bernice clapped her hands. 'Remember that night with the Wurlitzer and the Frogspawn Twins of Adaga III?'

'Oh my god, yes!'

'And then—' Other Bernice started, but the Doctor interrupted.

'Yes, well, that's all great and fun sounding. Now can we please get back to what we need to do here? Bernice, pack your bags and go home now.'

Bernice just laughed at his tone. 'What am I? Six? Or worse, still travelling with you? I need something better than that, Doctor. If that's truly who you are.'

Other Bernice stepped closer, but not close enough to touch. 'Remember when we were six. Remember Mum saying that if ever we needed to really trust in something, really believe in something, we were to remember her telling us this? Well, I'm thinking about that moment very strongly now. A chain of events starts with you digging here that a lot of Laws of Time-breaking has managed to avert.'

'And believe me, Bernice,' said the Doctor, 'you, I, Peter... many others barely got out of it. You have to believe me. Believe in yourself, quite literally. Leave this place and never come back.'

Bernice stared at the Doctor. His earnest face, those eyes, oh, always with those eyes... No matter how many times the face changed, the eyes stayed the same – weary, experienced, genuine. The Doctor she had loved for years, just as anyone who knew him did. Damn him. She turned to see if she could spot Jack and Ruth. They were little more than specks in the distance…

She turned back to Other Bernice and the Doctor.

They were gone.

Of course they were.

She had just made a decision. Time had already been rewritten, and things would unfold in a different way in the future and presumably the past.

Peter was at her side. 'I planted the explosives,' he said.

Bernice looked at him. 'Honey, go double them. Instead of uncovering this site, I want to bury it, make sure no one can ever try digging here again.'

'But…'

Bernice stroked his ears, kissed his forehead. 'Just do it, yeah?'

Peter smiled and hurried off.

An hour later she, Peter, Jack and Ruth were watching as the whole area vanished in a massive eruption of fire and rock – Peter smiled at his handiwork.

'You enjoyed that, didn't you?' Ruth said, nudging his ribs.

He nodded. 'Drinks on me, guys.'

They started back to their little shuttle ship, the *Irverfield*, and then back to Legion City.

As they got into the shuttle, Bernice turned and caught a glimpse of a tall blue box on the horizon. She blinked, but it was gone.

'Happy landings, Doctor,' she said quietly. 'Till the next time… Whatever face you may have…'

Endnote

So, it's all Steven Moffat's fault, you know. And I couldn't be more grateful to him!

I cheekily asked him if I could do a novel with River Song. He said no, so that it couldn't be contradicted by (or more importantly contradict) anything that may potentially happen with River and the Twelfth Doctor one day on the tellybox. And quite right too. 'But,' he said, 'put in Bernice. I like Bernice, you should bring her back.' And nothing brought a smile to my face more than that idea.

Not that long ago, myself and my sometime writing partner Scott Handcock had a fun couple of years doing Benny adventures on audio CD for Big Finish Productions. (A round of applause to them for saying yes to all this too, by the way.) We devised a new 'family' for her, bringing back her son Peter and creating Ruth and Jack. (The audios also featured the lovely Irving Braxiatel, but he was off doing some supply run for the White Rabbit or something equally dodgy with an Ikerian soft-furnishings merchant or a Surlioid spaceship dealer and wasn't available to take part in this adventure.) Scott and I stopped doing these after sixteen thrilling stories, but I truly love these characters, especially Benny, and so it took very little provocation (well, OK, none at all) to bring them all back together for this yarn, set some time after their last audio adventure.

I have to give a nod of the hat to those fine actors Lisa Bowerman, Tom Grant, Ayshea Antione-Brown and David Ames who brought Benny, Peter, Ruth and Jack to life so well. I heard their voices in my heads as I wrote each line of dialogue, and, if you're familiar with the audios, I hope you did too.

Finally a little yaaay too for the marvellous Peter Capaldi, who makes writing dialogue for his Doctor such a joy to do.

This book was mostly written in the spring of 2015 in Australia. Where it was actually autumn, moving towards winter. It gets very confusing for a poor feeble-minded Brit living down under try to understand these weird seasons. And don't get me started on the idea of celebrating Christmas Day in 70-degree heat on a beach. It's weird. Lovely. But dead weird… I have to say, if you've never visited the country, especially New South Wales, do yourself a favour and do so. It is amazing. Visit Sydney, of course, but I can't hype the breathtaking Blue Mountains enough. A day there is a day you'll never forget…

BBC

DOCTOR WHO

Royal Blood
Una McCormack

ISBN 978-1-101-90583-8

The Grail is a story, a myth! It didn't exist on your world! It can't exist here!

The city-state of Varuz is failing. Duke Aurelian is the last of his line, his capital is crumbling, and the armies of his enemy, Duke Conrad, are poised beyond the mountains to invade. Aurelian is preparing to gamble everything on one last battle. So when a holy man, the Doctor, comes to Varuz from beyond the mountains, Aurelian asks for his blessing in the war.

But all is not what it seems in Varuz. The city-guard have lasers for swords, and the halls are lit by electric candlelight. Aurelian's beloved wife, Guena, and his most trusted knight, Bernhardt, seem to be plotting to overthrow their Duke, and Clara finds herself drawn into their intrigue…

Will the Doctor stop Aurelian from going to war? Will Clara's involvement in the plot against the Duke be discovered? Why is Conrad's ambassador so nervous? And who are the ancient and weary knights who arrive in Varuz claiming to be on a quest for the Holy Grail…?

An original novel featuring the Twelfth Doctor and Clara, as played by Peter Capaldi and Jenna Coleman.

BBC

DOCTOR WHO

Deep Time
Trevor Baxendale

ISBN 978-1-101-90579-1

I do hope you're all ready to be terrified!

The Phaeron disappeared from the universe over a million years ago. They travelled among the stars using roads made from time and space, but left only relics behind. But what actually happened to the Phaeron? Some believe they were they eradicated by a superior force… Others claim they destroyed themselves.

Or were they in fact the victims of an even more hideous fate?

In the far future, humans discover the location of the last Phaeron road – and the Doctor and Clara join the mission to see where the road leads. Each member of the research team knows exactly what they're looking for – but only the Doctor knows exactly what they'll find.

Because only the Doctor knows the true secret of the Phaeron: a monstrous secret so terrible and powerful that it must be buried in the deepest grave imaginable…

An original novel featuring the Twelfth Doctor and Clara, as played by Peter Capaldi and Jenna Coleman